Jim Ryan joins a cattle drive from Texas along the Chisholm Trail to Abilene, Kansas. The story has all the adventure and excitement of the Old West, including storms and stampedes, horse thieves, a dāngerous river crossing, and, of course, the wild and unpredictable longhorn cattle themselves.

# Longhorns
# to
# Abilene

# BY PETER THOMSON

JACKET PAINTING AND CHAPTER DECORATION
BY GEORGE MOCNIAK

# Longhorns
# to
# Abilene

Follett Publishing Company • Chicago

LIBRARY OF CONGRESS CATALOG CARD NUMBER: 65-20064

123456789

*Dedicated to Maria K. Schneider*

# Longhorns
# to
# Abilene

# 1

The blazing Texas sun beat down on Jim Ryan with withering intensity, burning out his fast-waning strength. Gripping his saddle horn with both hands, he fought the giddiness which threatened to engulf him. Only one fact remained clear in his delirium-ridden mind: without help, he would perish in this endless sea of grass.

Jim had not passed a house within the last hundred miles; more than a week had elapsed since he had encountered a human being. Too weak to backtrack that distance, he rode on.

Thirst, hunger, and exhaustion sapped Jim's vitality until hope gave way to desperation and then to apathy. Slumped in his saddle, with head sagging, and his eyes

9

closed against the dazzling sun-glare, he swayed dizzily. His mount, aware that something was wrong, stopped walking.

"Giddap, Andy," Jim croaked. "Got to keep moving." He raised his head, opened his eyes and struggled for self-control. But the land tilted, his grip on the saddle horn loosened, and Jim lost consciousness before his body hit the ground.

Jim awoke in bed. Blinded by a shaft of sunlight that slanted through a small window directly into his eyes, he assumed that he was back in his mountain cabin.

He raised a hand to block out the glare and saw the bottom of a bunk a few inches above his face. Impulsively, he lurched out of bed. The instant his feet touched the floor, Jim felt faint. He swayed, staggered, and fell.

The door burst open and a small man hobbled into the room and awkwardly knelt beside Jim. He floundered, tried to stand up, but the little man lifted him back into the bunk with a surprising demonstration of strength.

"I'm all right. Let me up," Jim demanded.

"Easy, boy, don't be too proud to take help. I've doctored you for three days past, and you've still got no more strength than a just-dropped colt."

It made Jim uneasy to stay in bed while another man waited on him, but he was too weak to resist. "You say I've been here three days?" he asked.

"No, I brought you in last night. We was on the trail two days before that. It's a lucky thing I happened along when I did. From the looks of the mule tracks and droppings around you, I reckoned that you was downed for a day or two before I found you."

"How's Andy?"

"That'd be your mule. He's fat and shiny. The remuda elected him to take the place of the bell-mare we lost last month. They won't let him out of their sight."

"Thanks for taking care of him. I think a lot of old Andy. Since the war, he's all the family I've got. We grew up together, but he can still pull a plow with the best of them. He's a better saddle animal than any horse, back in the Great Smoky Mountains of Tennessee where good sense and sure-footedness count most."

"You've missed a lot of meals. Lay back for a spell and I'll rustle up a bait that'll put some meat back on your bones." The wiry little man limped out of the room.

The aroma and sound of a sizzling steak preceded the man through the door. Suddenly Jim was ravenously hungry. He sat up in bed and eagerly awaited the meal which would be his first in many days.

"You look anxious, young fella. Reckon this chow smells pretty good to a hungry man."

"You reckon right. A starving man thanks you."

"Don't mention it, boy. What do you want to be called?"

"I'm Jim Ryan."

The steak was fried cowboy style — well done, almost charred. It was not the tenderest piece of meat Jim had ever eaten, but he could not recall any that had tasted better.

He broke a fluffy biscuit and dabbed some sorghum

molasses on the top half. From the instant Jim popped the golden morsel into his mouth he knew that this was where he wanted to stay. He would have to work on another man's spread to learn how to gather cattle and drive them before he could go out on his own. Here was a cook who served up a man's kind of food — chow with flavor and with enough body to carry a man through a long day in the saddle. Jim swallowed a big mouthful of beans, sighed contentedly, then grinned amiably at the man who had first saved his life and then made it so pleasurable.

"Best bait I ever had," he said. "I don't know what kind of biscuits these are, and I never ate beans like these, but I sure like 'em."

"You've never et sourdough biscuits or pinto beans before?"

"Never in my put-together life."

"Stay in Texas and you'll eat just about nothin' else three meals a day for as long as you live."

"That suits me fine." Jim mopped up the last of the sorghum with a sourdough biscuit. "Your cooking would do me good from now on. What do you want to be called?"

The little cook grinned. "They call me Frisco, and I reckon that's just about as good a name as any for me. I made my strike in eighteen and forty-nine out in Californy and lost it all on the Barbary Coast in eighteen and fifty."

"That's a shame, Frisco. That's truly bad luck."

"It don't gall me. I was young and full of beans back then. I had fun gettin' it; losin' it was pretty interestin', too. I figure I came out even, and nobody got hurt."

"I guess you're right, Frisco. The main thing is, you wound up doing what you want to."

A shadow crossed Frisco's face, and Jim immediately changed the subject.

"Whose bunk am I in? Hadn't I better bed down in the barn?"

"Rest easy, Jim. This is my cookshack, and that's an extra bunk. You're welcome to stay as long as you're laid up."

"Any chance of getting work here?"

"Can't say, Jim. That's for the Old Man to decide. This is a small spread. Every hand on it has to pull his own weight and a little more."

"I'm a good worker, Frisco, maybe he'll put me on."

"Any experience handling cattle, or maybe horses, Jim?"

"No, I can't recall ever seeing more'n five cows at one time in my life. And that goes for horses, too."

"Then you'll likely have hard goin' here. But don't you fret about that right now." Frisco picked up the plate and cup and started to leave the room.

"Thanks, Frisco. Thanks for taking care of me and Andy. And I'm obliged for the bait. It really hit the spot!"

"Don't mention it, Jim." Frisco reached behind the door and brought out Jim's Kentucky rifle. "Here's another friend of yours I found out on the range."

Jim eagerly examined his weapon, looked at Frisco and smiled. "You've cleaned and oiled it for me, Frisco.

Thanks again. This old gun is sort of like my right arm — I grew up with it."

"We don't see many like that out here," Frisco said as he hobbled out of the room.

It was clear that Frisco saw little future out here in the cattle country for a young mountaineer with an old mule and a flintlock rifle. But Jim was confident. Having been second to none in the skills by which a man was measured back in his neck of the woods, he had no doubt that he could learn all he needed to know about handling cattle. Given time, he would ride the range with the best of them.

Like most mountain boys, Jim was a superb woodsman. He could measure a powder charge, ram ball and patch, powder the pan, and squeeze off a squirrel-barking shot in about a half-minute. A skilled hunter, trapper, and fisherman, Jim could live off the land with ease and comfort — when that land was his familiar woodland region. But how would that help him get a job here on the prairie?

Stories of this free, rich grassland and of herds of maverick longhorns had fascinated Jim and finally lured him to Texas. He had heard that there were thousands of unclaimed beeves to be had for the roping. A fellow could gather a herd, feed it for nothing on an open range, and drive it to Kansas, where the market was good. Men were making fortunes that way. Jim was sure that no such opportunity could be found in the Tennessee wilderness. Things were not good back there after the war. Maybe it wouldn't be easy to get started here, but it had to be better than where Jim came from. All he needed was a place to start and time to learn.

Experimentally, he sat up and swung his legs out over the side of the bunk. He was steadier than he expected to be. Gingerly, he stood up, then slowly walked to the window. For miles, he could see nothing but a vast expanse of Texas prairie. There were no trees, no building was in sight, and in all that area he saw no cattle. There was nothing but grass as far as the eye could see.

Crossing the room, he looked through another window and saw a low, solid-looking adobe ranch house. There was another outbuilding that looked like a storehouse. Frisco had called this a small spread, but it looked good to Jim.

Wanting to get dressed and go out for a look around, he turned and walked back toward the bunk. But his ordeal had drained Jim's strength. He staggered, flopped onto the bed, and just managed to pull the blanket over himself before he fell asleep.

## 2

Jim slept like a hibernating bear, even during the noisy arrival of the ranch hands and through their departure the following morning. It was almost noon when he awoke.

"Why didn't you roll me out, Frisco?" he asked. "I don't want to sleep my life away."

"The sleep did you good — you look like a new man," Frisco answered. "Chow'll be waitin' when you're ready. The wash rack's out there, just beyond the door."

Jim dressed quickly. He was feeling fit and eager to see what there was to be seen on the cattle ranch. There was a bucket of water on the wash bench and a half dozen tin basins hanging from nails of the rack. He filled one of them, washed his hands and face and dried them on the clean roller towel. Then he washed and rinsed the basin and hung it back on the rack.

He paused for a moment to look around. The buildings were made of thick adobe clay bricks. There was very little wood anywhere. The wash bench and rack were built of cottonwood poles, as was the hitching rack. There were three very small trees that obviously had been brought from some distance and planted by someone who was anxious to bring a little shade to this prairie ranch. They had been watered that morning.

Back where Jim had lived trees grew all around and men had to clear the land before planting. When a mountain man needed a cabin, a fence, a crib, or a coffin, he began by whetting his ax. In this prairie region there was no use for axes or for men who were skilled in their use. Jim smiled ruefully at the realization that this was one more ability which would be of no value here.

"What do you think of the place?" Frisco asked, as Jim came into the cookshack.

"Looks good to me, what I saw of it. But I reckon I don't know what to look for on a ranch, this being the first one I ever saw."

"It's like most of 'em in this neighborhood. Not much better than most, not much worse than some."

"What do you call a neighborhood? I didn't see another house in any direction, and you can see a long way in this country."

"I reckon our nearest neighbor is the M N X spread, about twenty miles west of here."

"M N X," Jim said. "Are those the owner's initials?"

"No, the owner is Nate Barnes. Right after the war, when steers sold for a couple of dollars a head, Nate lived on nothing but beef for a long spell — and so did a lot of others in these parts.

"One day a friend asked him how he was gettin' along, and Nate said that he'd gladly swap the whole kit-and-caboodle for a plate of ham and eggs. The word got around, and from then on, the Nate Barnes spread was called the Ham and Eggs Ranch. Old Nate went along with the joke and registered the M N X brand."

"What's our brand, Frisco?"

"This place belongs to Tom Peters, and his brand looks like this." Frisco pulled a large silver watch out of his pocket and handed it to Jim, backside up, to reveal an engraved replica of the ranch brand:

Jim studied it carefully. "I can't figure it out," he finally admitted. "I reckon this brand has a story behind it, too."

"No, it's his initials."

"His initials? I can't see how a wigwam ties in with T.P. . . ." Jim caught on as soon as the words were spoken. "Oh," he said weakly.

"You'll see the Tepee brand on the left hip of all

our cattle and on the left shoulder of our horses. And you'll find it on just about everything else on the ranch."

"Like your watch."

"That was a gift from the Old Man," Frisco said without elaboration.

"What can I do for you? I'd like to earn my keep."

"A man who's sick or hungry doesn't pay for hospitality on the Tepee spread, nor on any other ranch around here," Frisco growled.

"No offense intended, but I'm strong and willing, and so's Andy. I'd consider it a favor if you'd let me make myself useful around here in any way I can."

"Jim, there's nothin' needs doin', take my word for it. I've plenty to do, though, and you'd just get in my way. But I'm obliged to you for askin'."

"Thanks for another good handout, Frisco," Jim said. "Reckon I'll ride out and see what a cattle ranch looks like."

Eagerly he walked toward the small corral where his mule was confined with about a dozen saddle horses.

As Jim approached, Andy pranced to the gate bars and greeted him with an ear-shattering bray that was music to his young master's ears. The cow ponies watched every move the old mule made, as though they were ready to follow him anywhere, but Andy ignored them and stretched his neck until his big head was far beyond the top rail.

As the youth scratched one of the mule's long, hairy ears and then the other, Andy leaned against the corral bars with his eyes closed and his lower lip hanging pendulously in an idiotic expression of happiness.

Jim chuckled as he caressed the old mule, "Why you broomtailed, knobby-kneed, pot-bellied, hammerheaded old mountain canary! You ought to be ashamed. Don't you know that mules are cantankerous, mean, and stubborn? You're supposed to be rough, tough, and hard to bluff. Here you are, acting like a kitten full of cream."

Jim decided to ride bareback. He bridled Andy, lowered the corral gate bars and waved back a couple of horses that tried to follow the mule out.

"We'd have a job getting those feisty critters back once they headed out for the open range, Andy."

Lifelong habit made him take along his rifle. He would rather leave without breakfast than without it or the sheath knife which hung from his belt.

Holding the rifle in his left hand, he clutched a fistful of Andy's coarse mane and vaulted upon the mule's broad back.

Jim clamped his long legs around Andy's barrel for a moment, then relaxed and let his feet dangle as he rode toward the river.

Andy stopped at the water's edge to assure himself that the footing was firm, then waded to midstream where he could stand belly-deep in the water for easy drinking.

Critically, he sniffed the water, then tasted it. Unlike a horse, Andy drank slowly, hesitantly; and while he drank his ears were never still. They scanned the area for unfamiliar sounds which might indicate danger during the brief period when he could see little and smell almost nothing. Suddenly his ears stopped waving, pointed upstream, and his head swung up violently. He snorted to clear the water from his nostrils.

For a few seconds, Jim could neither see nor hear anything unusual, but he had learned to heed Andy's re- actions — a habit which had served him well more than a few times in the past.

Attracted by a movement in the distance, he saw a mounted man. Both horse and rider were dwarfed by distance, but they grew fast as the horse galloped toward the river. The rider quirted his mount into a dead run. What made the man drive his horse so hard? Maybe he needed help, but Jim could see no one pursuing him.

The cowboy rode up to the edge of the river, faced Jim, and glared at him with a hostile arrogance that irri- tated the proud young mountaineer who was already nettled by the way the rider had abused his fine, sensitive looking horse. Jim bristled as the cowboy sized him up, but he did not waver under the horseman's cold appraisal.

He was about twenty years old, of medium height, powerfully built; with broad shoulders, deep chest, and the slim legs and small hips of a man who has spent more hours in the saddle than on his feet. His black Stetson sombrero must have cost him a month's pay, Jim thought, and his handsome, fancy-stitched boots could not have cost very much less. This fellow's vanity was revealed in everything he wore and in the beautiful saddle in which he rode.

Jim was acutely aware of his own ragged clothing and of what a completely unimpressive figure he pre- sented — mounted on an old mule, bareback, and carrying a rifle that must look like a relic to men of these parts.

He felt his cheeks growing hot under the cowboy's contemptuous stare, and his anger drove him into a stubborn determination not to falter. He locked his opponent's blue eyes with a level gaze. Jim was now too angry to consider the foolishness of his pride — he came from a region where fierce pride is akin to honor.

Jim was a friendly youth, but he had a stubborn streak which had brought him more than his share of trouble. Now his anger was dangerously near the boiling point. In the heat of this silent conflict with the arrogant stranger, he failed to notice the approach of another man until a voice cut through the ominous silence.

"What's the trouble here, Curly?"

The cowboy swung around to face the newcomer. "This ringy tramp's pleadin' to get stomped, and I've half a mind to oblige."

"You've got a big mouth," Jim snapped. "I'm not looking for trouble, but I reckon I can handle anything you've got in that half a mind of yours."

"Hold it!" the third man commanded. "Both of you stop right now!"

He spoke with the authority of one who is accustomed to giving orders. Even in his angry mood, Jim obeyed without hesitation.

The man was about forty years old, tall, rangy, and competent looking. He rode out into the river and looked at Jim closely for a moment. Then he smiled.

"You must be the dogie that Frisco found out on the range," he said.

Jim did not know what a dogie was, but he liked the tone of the man's voice and the warmth of his smile, so he accepted the greeting as a friendly one. "I reckon I've been your uninvited guest for a long time, sir," he said. "I want to work out my keep, if you'll let me."

"Out here we don't accept pay for helping a man, son. What do you want to be called?"

"My name's Jim Ryan, sir."

"You can forget the 'sir.' I'm Tom Peters." The rancher pulled off his right gauntlet and extended a white, soft-skinned hand which surprised Jim, who was accustomed to the brown, calloused hands of the mountain men.

"Curly," Tom Peters called, "come over here and shake hands with — "

The cowboy jerked the reins, spinning his horse around in a hard turn. The horse broke into a dead run and carried Curly over the prairie at a breakneck speed.

Tom Peters watched the angry rider and shook his head. The rancher obviously was disgusted, but he said nothing to Jim about it.

"Ever worked on a ranch, Jim?" he asked as his horse joined Andy in a drink of the river water.

"Never. This is the first time I've ever been on one. I'd work for nothing but my keep while I learn, if you could see your way clear to give me a chance."

"No man works without pay on the Tepee spread, Jim, but every man really earns his money here. I don't know whether I can use you or not. Stay on a few days as our guest, then we'll see."

Tom Peters rode toward the ranch house, and Jim rode along with him as far as the corral. He did not care for the idea of staying as a non-working guest, but it was better than moving on to a new place. Here he had at least one friend who might put in a good word for him.

Frisco stood at the door of the cookshack. He greeted Jim with a wave as he walked up from the corral.

"I see you met the Old Man, Jim," Frisco said, referring to a man who probably was more than ten years his junior.

"Yes, I met him at the river. He invited me to stay here a couple of days while he makes up his mind about me."

"And you wonder how you can make him decide to hire you?"

"That's about the size of it, Frisco. I offered to work for just my keep until I learn what it's all about, but he said every man on this spread works for pay or he doesn't work at all. That cuts my chance down to a nub. I'm sure worthless on a cattle ranch right now." Jim grinned at Frisco.

"That gives us until the day after tomorrow to make a cowhand outa you," Frisco said. "The Old Man and Curly are goin' out again this afternoon. They'll be gone a couple days with the rest of the boys. We'll have the place to ourselves until then, and I'll see what I can do for you."

"I'll sure be obliged to you, Frisco."

"I doubt that. You'll be too beat up to thank me two days from now. I don't give you a faint chance of makin' it, but if you're game, I'm willin' to do what I can."

"I'm game, Frisco. And I thank you in advance."

Jim ate his noon meal in the cookshack with Tom Peters. Curly was seated at the same table with them, but he might as well have been in another county. He said nothing to Tom Peters or Jim during the entire meal.

"How do you feel today, Jim?" the rancher asked. "I hear you had a pretty rough time of it."

"I feel fine, thanks, Mr. Peters. Frisco took good care of me. I haven't felt this spry since I left the hills."

"You're a long way from home."

"I'm not in any trouble back there, Mr. Peters. My father was killed in the war, and we lost our farm. Then my mother took sick and died, and I lived with neighbors for a couple of years. As soon as I turned sixteen, I decided to pull out. I couldn't see any future for me."

"Do you think you have a good future here — in a strange country where everything is different?"

"This is a growing country, and I'm growing, too. I figure there has to be a place somewhere in the West for me and for a lot of other fellows like me. I sure aim to find mine, and I hope it's right here."

"You admit you don't know cattle. You've never been on a ranch before so you can't handle a rope, break a horse, or brand a calf. What can you do, Jim?"

"I can learn, Mr. Peters. I can learn to do anything that needs doing; just like I learned to handle a mule — either plowin' or packin'. I can shoot my rifle, and I'm a good hunter."

Curly snorted.

Angrily, Jim half-rose to challenge the cowboy, but he decided against it. Too much was at stake right now to risk Tom Peters' displeasure by a show of his hot temper.

The rancher glanced at Curly, then at Jim, but he made no comment.

"I don't know how we could make much use of plowing, hunting, or rifle shooting, Jim. Don't get your hopes set on working here, but we'll talk about it when I get back. So long; see you in a couple of days."

Tom Peters and Curly took their plates and utensils out to the kitchen and put them into the dishpan. They pulled on their gauntlets and put on their sombreros before stepping out into the sunshine. The only three men Jim had met in the cattle country were marked by white hands and foreheads, as though they never went outside without hats and gloves.

Frisco came back into the dining room as Jim finished his last mouthful. Jim picked up his plate and utensils and put them into the pan, as the others had. Frisco refused his offer to help with the dishes, so he went outside and waited for the cook to finish his chores.

Two days! He had only two days to learn enough about ranching to convince Tom Peters that he would be of value to him — to start from scratch with only a cook to instruct him. But Jim did not allow himself to admit the possibility of failure. He was determined to work for the Tepee brand because he liked Frisco, admired Tom Peters, and because he wanted to show Curly a thing or two.

3

"First you've got to catch 'em," Frisco said as he shook out his lariat. "Out in Californy, I've seen Mexican cowboys — vaqueros, they call themselves — use reatas sixty to eighty feet long."

"What's a reata, Frisco?"

"It's their name for a rope made out of braided rawhide. *La reata.* That's where our word lariat came from.

"They can throw a wide loop fifty or sixty feet while chousin' a steer through horse-high chaparral brush and drop it around the critter with nary a miss. A quick dally around the saddle horn secures the free end of the reata, and the vaquero has caught hisself a steer.

"The pony squats, takes root, and dumps the steer,

27

pronto. It's a beautiful sight to behold, but it takes years to get the hang of the long reata. There ain't many dally boys in Texas, except some Mexican vaqueros. If you ever get a chance to see one of 'em in action, don't pass it up."

"I won't, Frisco," Jim answered, "but how does a Texan handle a rope?"

"Hard-and-fast. Nothin' fancy. Your Texan ties the end of a thirty-foot grass rope fast to his saddle horn and rides down on top of a critter, dabs a loop over its horns, and pulls up the slack. Then he flips the string over the steer's back and cuts the other way — jerkin' the critter's hoofs out from under him."

"You make it sound easy. Easy and dangerous," Jim said.

"It's a mite tricky," Frisco admitted. "You want to be workin' a horse with savvy. A longhorn steer tied hard-and-fast can spell trouble if your horse don't throw him."

Frisco casually cast his loop over a hitching post twenty feet away. "The trick," he said, "is to keep your loop flat and drop it over your target. Then pull it up so the rope runs through the honda — that's the eye — and closes the loop. Try it."

Jim retrieved the rope and gathered it into coils about twenty inches in diameter. Then he formed a wide loop and, holding the rope about eight inches from the honda, he cast it at the post. It began well, but the loop abruptly stopped in midair and dropped to the ground about five feet from his toes.

"You started out fine, but your left hand didn't know what your right was doin'. You forgot to play out the slack."

Frisco coiled his lariat and built a loop. He showed Jim how to hold the coils in his left hand and release his fingers as the rope left his hand so it would run over three fingers as it played out, allowing it to run freely but under control.

"Nothin' to it," he said.

"Of course not; any child can do it," Jim answered wryly. He continued to practice, trying to play the rope out from his left hand as he threw the loop with his right. His first few tries were awkward, but he improved with each attempt and soon was able to keep the loop clear and wide as he threw it.

"That's good. That's fine," Frisco said encouragingly, after he had corrected several of Jim's mistakes.

Then Jim dropped his loop over the post for the first time, and he was sure that he had learned the knack of it. Before long, he was averaging eight catches out of ten throws.

"You're gettin' the hang of it," Frisco said. "You'll make a roper yet."

Jim's confidence increased with each good throw. Trailing the lariat, he walked toward the post and neatly dropped his loop over it with a twenty-foot throw.

"Good work!" Frisco said. "That's the way you'll have to come up to your mount every morning. Just drag your loop, keep it wide and clear so you can dab it over his head in one easy swing. It sure beats the showy, looptwirlin', horse-scarin' throw some of the boys favor."

"Don't you ever swing the loop over your head before you throw it?" Jim asked.

"Swing it high when you're chousin' a steer through the brush — you can't drag a string then. But for catchin' your pony in a corral, you'd better not swing your loop. Now let's try it on your mule."

"I can't do that, Frisco."

"Why not? You've got to learn how to dab your loop over a critter. There's not much work on this spread for a hitchin'-post roper."

"Don't get me wrong. I'm ready to try it out on a live critter, but not on old Andy. He's never been roped, and he's never gonna be. When I want him I whistle, and he ambles up like a pet dog."

Frisco looked long and hard at his young pupil. "So that hammerheaded old mule's too good to be handled like a horse."

"Not a bit, but he's too good to be abused by a fellow he trusts. I hate to stand up against you, but I won't do that to Andy even for you."

"I'm not askin' you to. You won your argument the first time you said no."

There were about a dozen ponies in the corral. Pointing their ears toward the approaching pair, they momentarily eyed the rope which Jim was dragging in the dust, then they wheeled and milled to the far side of the corral. It was hard for Jim to find a target among the rope-wise cow ponies as they bunched together with their heads down and their rumps pointed toward him.

"They don't cooperate worth a hoot, do they, Jim?"

"Not a little bit. Which one shall I try for?"

"The little blaze-faced bay."

Jim ducked between the bars of the corral and advanced on the milling horses without the haziest idea of how to get them spread out so he could cast his loop at the one Frisco had pointed out. As though sensing his intentions, the cow pony backed away to keep several of the other horses between himself and the would-be cowboy. Even old Andy cocked an ear at his master as though questioning his sanity.

After checking his loop, Jim advanced on his quarry with infinite patience, developed through years of stalking wary forest animals. The smart pony was equally patient, making it difficult for Jim to gain an advantage. But as he advanced, he was ever alert for a break, and when the other horses suddenly bolted away from his target, he took advantage of the fleeting opportunity and lassoed the bay like an expert.

Jim braced himself as the rope settled around the neck of the fast-moving pony, but the bay stopped the instant he felt the rope.

The other horses moved away as Jim walked, hand-over-hand, down the rope. He patted the handsome animal's neck and then led him to the gate as Frisco dropped the bars.

"He sure fooled me," Jim said. "I expected him to drag me all around the corral, but he came along like a leashed hound."

"They soon learn not to fight the rope," Frisco said.

"Those little cow ponies are long on savvy."

"Is he a mustang?" Jim asked.

"No, a mustang's a wild horse. This one comes from good quarter horse stock — the best breed there is for this work. He's tough, fast, and smart — and mighty rugged. For a short way, he can outrun any racehorse, and, if he's handled right, he can outmaneuver the spookiest steer alive. You'll see what I mean if you stay on this ranch long. But right now, your job is to get on this pony and see how you can handle him."

"I don't claim to be a broncobuster, Frisco."

"He don't need bustin'. He needs a good workin' pardner."

Jim slipped Andy's bridle on the bay and adjusted it for a better fit.

Frisco shook his head doubtfully as he watched Jim put his beat-up old saddle on the bay. The first longhorn to throw his half-ton of steel-muscled fury against a rope tied to that saddle's horn would pull it out by the roots.

Jim held the reins and the saddle horn in both hands and vaulted into the saddle without touching his toe to the stirrup. He saw the astonished look on Frisco's face and laughed.

"What do I do now?" Jim asked.

"Hanged if I know. I never thought to see anybody mount like that — without he was a Ay-rab. Why did you let on you couldn't handle a horse?"

"That's the way I mount Andy. I ride him bareback a lot, but I don't know what to do now that I'm up here."

"To begin with, these ponies are broke to neck-rein.

Hold both ribbons light and high in your left hand. If
you want to turn right, just pass your left hand with the
reins over to the right above his neck and he'll go thataway. Put a little pressure against his side with your left
knee at the same time. Some ponies can be guided with
nothing but knee pressure. A good cow pony will usually
follow either signal."

"Giddap!" Jim commanded.

The horse did not move. Frisco gave his pupil such a
pained look that Jim laughed in spite of his embarrass-
ment.

"Cow ponies don't savvy giddap, nor whoa, nor gee,
nor haw. Save that lingo for mules, oxen, and eastern
horses. Now, loosen them ribbons and touch your heel
to his flank, and he'll go. Pull up on the reins, and he'll
stop."

Jim touched the bay's flank with his right heel, and
the animal responded like a hair-triggered rifle. From a
dead stop, he reached a full gallop in a single jump. Jim
would have been unseated if the horse had not moved so
smoothly.

"Whoa!" he yelled, forgetting Frisco's instructions.
"Whoa! Whoa!"

The fiery little quarter horse increased his speed.
Jim yanked on one rein and then the other, trying to turn
the running horse.

The outraged bay clamped the bit between his strong
jaws, tossed his head to free the reins, then ducked it
between his forelegs and humped his powerful back.

Up he went, sunfishing, arching his body first to one

33

side and then to the other. Jim didn't have a chance. He reached for the horn, missed it, and was thrown to the ground with a sickening thud.

Stunned, he lay still for a moment, shook his head to clear out the ringing noises, painfully rose to his feet and hobbled over to the quietly grazing pony.

"You hurt, Jim?" Frisco asked.

"I think I'll live. I'm not sure I want to, but I'll live. What'd I do wrong?"

"Everything. Absolutely everything! I told you how to turn him and stop him, but you paid me no heed. You sawed that poor critter's mouth, yanking them reins like you did, and he dumped you like any self-respecting cow pony would."

Jim patted the bay's neck. "I didn't mean to hurt you, boy, and you sure paid me back for it. Let's give it another try, just like it never happened."

"First let me show you how to mount like a cowboy instead of a jumping jack. Then maybe he won't be so upset to begin with."

"I aim to please, Frisco. If you and this horse don't like the way I mount, I'll change to suit. How do I do it?"

Frisco was too badly crippled to demonstrate, but neither he nor Jim mentioned the fact.

"A cow pony lights out when a man's left foot hits the stirrup. Face the rear, and his motion will swing you up into the saddle. Hang onto his mane, your reins, and the horn with your left hand, and grab the horn with your right, too. Swing up easylike, but get your right foot into the stirrup fast. You've got no control without you're tight in the saddle; so get that way right off."

Frisco looked at Jim's shoes and shook his head.

"If you're goin' to be a cowboy, you'd better get hold of some cash money and get the right gear. Those clodhoppers of yours might do fine for pursuin' a plow, but they sure don't belong out here in the cattle country."

Jim started to speak, then clamped his jaws shut to hold back the angry reply that came to mind. Frisco had no call to remind him that he was penniless and shabby. But Frisco was his friend and benefactor, so Jim kept quiet. Instead of speaking, he looked with new interest at Frisco's boots. U. S. 1331927

"Pointed toes get your feet into the stirrups fast," Frisco explained, "and the high heels keep 'em from goin' on through. The right boots save many a rider from hangin' up and gettin' dragged to death when his saddle turns or he gets tossed off his bronc. High heels help a man dig in when he's roped a calf from the ground."

Jim was going to have a pair of boots like that someday. His pride had been damaged by Curly's reaction to his shabby appearance. He knew that he needed boots, a new saddle, and some presentable clothes. More than ever, he was determined to get a job quickly and earn the money he needed to properly outfit himself.

He followed Frisco's instruction and, just as the cowboy-cook had predicted, the pony lit out the moment Jim's left toe touched the stirrup, swinging him up into the saddle. He groped for the right stirrup for an instant, located it, and sat in the saddle with the feeling of control over his spirited mount.

He reined the pony leftward and circled back toward Frisco. The little bay responded beautifully, so Jim lightly reined him to the opposite direction. Encouraged by the cow pony's obedience to his most subtle silent commands, he stopped using the reins; just held them above the animal's neck and leaned to the right slightly as he pressed his left knee against the saddle. The horse responded perfectly. He rode back to where Frisco waited.

"This horse is better than most, isn't he?"

"He's the best in my string, and he's about as good a cutting pony as you'll find on this spread."

"He's wonderful," Jim said, "full of spirit and good sense. Now I'm sorrier than ever that I abused him, but he doesn't appear to be holding a grudge."

"You might get to be pretty good with a horse. You've got a lot to learn — just about everythin' there is to know about a cow pony — but you've got patience workin' for you. Guess that comes from handlin' mules."

Jim grinned. "Glad I've got something working for me."

"Why not take a ride, Jim? You and the bay'll get along fine as long as you remember what you've learned."

"I'll sure work on it, Frisco. What's his name?"

"Dancer. He's a smooth little traveler, and he knows how to handle hisself, if you give him his head. Remember, if you get into trouble and don't know what to do next, you can usually make out by lettin' a good cow pony have his way about it."

# 4

Dancer was well named. Given a light hand on the reins, he moved with an easy gait that could cover a lot of miles in a short time with a minimum of wear and tear on himself or his rider. After riding a couple of hours, Jim estimated that they had traveled a good ten miles. He scanned the rolling terrain where prairie grass grew horsebelly high. This was good, rich grazing land, but he had yet to see his first bull, steer, cow, or calf in a region where he had expected to find a thousand head of cattle.

Without guidance, Dancer veered toward a distant clump of cottonwood trees which was the only landmark within sight.

As they neared the prairie oasis, Jim was startled by

an ear-shattering bellow. Before he could determine its source, his mount broke into a run, circled the grove and stopped just short of a steer that was trapped belly deep in a bog.

The unfortunate brute had lost none of its fierce temper. As Jim approached, the longhorn rolled his eyes and roared — a ferocious bellow of frustrated rage.

Jim had never seen such magnificent weapons on any animal as this longhorn's long, sharp horns, which must have spanned six feet from tip to tip. But the lean, angular beast looked as though all of his growth had been concentrated on those immense horns. It was long all the way — long-horned, long-necked, and long-faced. Jim was sure that its submerged body was built along the same lines, and he wondered how he could pull so large an animal, with such loose-looking joints, out of the bog without tearing it limb from limb.

Despite his lack of experience, he did not hesitate. It might be too late if he rode back for help.

Building a large loop, he easily tossed it over the steer's long horns on his first cast. He pulled in the slack until the loop closed over the base of the steer's horns and then mounted Dancer for the pullout.

Jim tied the end of the rope to his saddle horn with a double half-hitch. He was about ready to get Dancer started when it occurred to him that he had better check his cinch. He dismounted and tightened it a little so the strain would not pull the saddle around under Dancer's belly.

The saddle was very old, and the cinch and latigo

straps, which had never been designed for this kind of work, looked worn and weak. Jim was dubious about his ability and about the capacity of his equipment for this job, but he had to try. The steer was neck deep in the bog and might go all the way under if Jim did not hurry.

Remounting, he held the reins lightly but without slack. The steer braced his neck against the rope, glared at Jim with hostile red eyes, and shook his fearsomely armed head with a ferocity that made Jim look at the rifle which he had leaned against a nearby tree. He was tempted to go back and get it — just in case.

He decided against it, clucked, and touched Dancer's flank with his heel.

Dancer knew exactly what to do. Undaunted by the menacing steer or by the inexperience of his rider, he pulled with gradually increasing power. Jim could feel the stress against his old saddle, but he gave Dancer his head. Even as he suspected that his cinch was beginning to break, he felt the forward progress of Dancer's digging hoofs. The steer began to emerge.

Dancer crouched and strained harder against the steer's weight. Step by step, the cow pony pulled the big longhorn out of the mire. Then, with a lurch, the steer exploded out of the bog — a thousand pounds of fury ready to attack anything that moved.

The range-wise horse, anticipating this action, reacted with speed and courage. The rope tied him to the frenzied steer, but he used it as an offensive weapon rather than as a handicap. Without unseating his rider, Dancer raced ahead of the infuriated steer to a place where the ground was firm and level before he stopped.

The longhorn lowered his head and charged on a straight line. Dancer wheeled, let the animal pass, then stopped, braced his forelegs and planted his hoofs into the ground.

The slack rope ran between the steer's forelegs and, as it snapped taut against the weight of the braced cow pony, the charging longhorn flipped hoofs over horns, swapped ends, and landed on his back.

Dancer stepped back and kept the rope tight to counter any attempt by the steer to regain his feet. The cow pony seemed to be waiting for his rider to take charge.

Jim had been nothing more than a passenger trying to stay in the saddle during the conflict between the two animals, but the time had come for him to act.

When he had roped the steer, Jim had not thought out the problem of how a lone man could disengage his lariat loop from the wide-spreading horns of a furious steer. The problem came to his mind as Dancer was upending the longhorn, but he did not consider letting it get away with Frisco's rope still attached to its horns.

Now, with the steer on its back, he could see only one way to solve the problem without killing the steer or cutting the lariat. Acting with more courage than knowhow, Jim leaped from Dancer's back and ran along the lariat. The steer was an awesome creature close up, with those tremendous horns gleaming in the sunlight and his muscular body thrashing wildly. The enraged steer seemed all horns and hoofs — lashing out in all directions.

Jim was afraid of the dangerous animal, but he was too busy to think about that as he lunged in, past the flailing hoofs, and grabbed the terrible horns in both hands. Then, not knowing what to do next, he sat on the steer's long neck to pin him down.

Dancer continued to brace himself against the lariat, and Jim did not know how to make the pony ease off. He needed some slack rope so he could loosen the loop and remove it.

"Here, Dancer!" he called, as he fought to hold the steer down. He clucked to attract the cow pony, but there was no reaction.

"Giddap, Dancer!" he yelled. Again there was no response.

He grabbed the rope and gave it a couple of hard jerks. That worked. Whether it was the right signal or whether Dancer had become aware of the problem, Jim neither knew nor cared at that moment. Quickly, he slipped the honda to enlarge the loop and removed it from the horns of the struggling steer.

Jim had a tiger by the tail. As long as he sat on the steer's neck, he could hold it down, but he knew what would happen the instant he released the dangerous brute. The longhorn was mad at the world in general and at Jim and Dancer in particular. There was no doubt in Jim's mind but that, once released, the longhorn would gore him before he could mount Dancer.

The lariat was his only weapon, but he was determined not to cut it. Dancer was closer now and there was plenty of slack in the rope. But how could he release the infuriated animal before he was mounted on Dancer?

Then Jim thought of a hitch that he had frequently used to tie Andy to a post — a secure knot which could be released by a single jerk on the loose end of the rope. That just might do the trick!

Still sitting on the writhing steer's neck and gripping one of its horns with his left hand, he tossed the rope over the animal's forelegs, pulled it around them, just below the knees, and hung on for all he was worth. Forming a bight with the running end of the rope, he looped it over the standing part, drew the doubled rope around and through the bight and drew it tight. Then he was all set.

Holding the slipknot in place, he jerked on the lariat, and Dancer responded by backing up and bracing himself. Slowly, Jim eased his weight off the steer's neck, ready to jump back upon him if necessary. Making certain that the end of the rope was clear of the steer, he sprinted to the horse, vaulted into the saddle, and touched his heels to Dancer's flanks.

The steer furiously fought the rope as soon as it was slackened, and, for a suspenseful moment, Jim feared that it would regain its feet. But the slipknot held, and the animal flopped down again.

Jim walked Dancer to the steer's head, hesitated apprehensively as the animal hooked at him, then he reached across its neck and jerked the loose end of the lariat.

As the hitching tie dropped off, the enraged steer bellowed, leaped to its feet in a single bound, and furiously lunged at Dancer. But the nimble cow pony stepped aside. The steer wheeled and again charged, missed, wheeled and charged a third time. Each time Dancer agilely evaded him. Finally, the tiring steer, weakened by his ordeal in the bog, bellowed a parting threat and hightailed into the tall grass.

"Whew!" Jim said as he dismounted to get his rifle. After checking it, he mounted and went on his way again.

Hearing hoofbeats, he turned in the saddle, thinking that the steer was again attacking him. But it was another horseman, coming up fast. Jim gripped his rifle, ready for trouble, but the approaching rider raised his right hand high in the universal gesture of peaceful intent.

"Howdy, pilgrim," the cowboy said, as he reined his mount to a halt. "I figured you could use a little help, but I got here too late."

"Thanks, anyway. I made out all right — thanks to a smart little horse and a lot of luck." Jim grinned at the stranger. He noted the small Tepee brand on the left shoulder of the cowboy's horse and knew that this was one of Tom Peters' riders.

"I'm Jim Ryan," he said. "Frisco found me, more dead than alive, out on the prairie and brought me back to the land of the living. He gave me the loan of his pony," Jim explained in case the cowboy might think that he had stolen the blaze-faced bay.

"I heard about you. I'm Ace Dawson." He removed his right glove and extended a strong, white hand. They shook hands without dismounting.

Jim liked the looks of the fair-haired, blue-eyed cowboy. His smile was pleasant, and his face showed strength as well as friendliness.

"If you don't mind a friendly tip," Ace said, "pulling bog ain't the safest game a man can play all by himself — especially a greenhorn. You might do well to go for help next time, Jim."

"Any tip you can give me will be appreciated. I'm gonna be making a mess of mistakes while I'm learning."

"I'm outriding. Come along if you've a mind to."

Jim was interested in Ace's outfit, as well as in the man himself. His pants were dark blue wool, pegged at the calves so they could be tucked into his boot tops without bulging too much. His boots were soft-topped, beautifully stitched, narrow-toed, high-heeled, and very thin-soled.

He wore no belt. His woolen shirt was also blue, and a red bandanna was folded diagonally, tied with a square knot, and draped around his neck.

The wide-brimmed black sombrero was high-crowned, with four big dimples shaped into the top and decorated with a braided horsehair band.

Behind the cantle of his heavy, double-cinched saddle, tied with leather thongs, was a yellow poncho which bulged with other objects rolled inside of it. A neatly coiled lariat hung from a thong at the right side of the saddle horn. A booted carbine lay flat under the right stirrup with its butt facing forward — quickly accessible but out of the way of both rider and horse. Like the man, his equipment was serviceable, practical, ready for action.

Ace rode in long stirrups, as though standing rather than sitting in his saddle. He scanned the prairie constantly, and Jim was sure that very little of what was out there escaped the notice of his sombrero-shaded eyes.

They waded their horses out into the river where the animals could drink comfortably.

"I haven't seen any cattle, except the bogged steer," Jim said. "Where's the herd?"

"There are several herds," Ace said. "Right now we're holding 'em for the drive north."

Seeing the puzzled expression on Jim's face, he explained, "This is an open range. Four different outfits graze their cattle around here, so when an owner wants to brand his calves or sell a herd, he has to round up his cattle. We just finished gathering ours, branding the calves, and cutting out the steers to be sold.

"The Old Man is putting twelve hundred head on the trail to Abilene in a few days. We rounded them up, and we've got the whole gather in a holding spot — a box canyon about fifteen miles west of here."

"You're going to walk more'n a thousand head of wild longhorns, like the monster I tangled with, all the way to Abilene? Why that must be all of five hundred miles from here!"

"Give or take a hundred; depending on the way you go."

Jim didn't see how they could drive the longhorns one mile, if they all acted like the one he had battled. But, remembering how Dancer had performed, and thinking about men like Frisco, Ace, Curly, and Tom Peters,

Jim thought that maybe the right men, mounted on the right horses, could do the job. What an adventure that would be! He just had to go along with them.

"What's this outriding, Ace?" he asked.

"Troubleshooting, looking for strays, checking bogs. Mostly, you figure all the ways cattle can get into trouble and do what you can to keep 'em from it — or get 'em out of it."

"Thanks for letting me ride along with you, Ace. I'd better be heading back to the ranch before Frisco figures that I've laid me down on the prairie again."

"You can learn a lot from Frisco if you listen more'n you talk. He was the best hand this outfit ever had, before he got himself all stove-up last fall. So long, Jim."

"So long, Ace."

The ride back to the ranch passed without incident, but with plenty of interest. A gaunt coyote ghosted through the distant mesquite, his shabby gray-brown fur blending into the brush. He flanked Jim on a parallel course just out of rifle range, as though his curiosity was exactly balanced by his cunning timidity.

A Texas jackrabbit, all legs and ears, saw the coyote, stopped, and disappeared as his thin body blended with perfect camouflage against the prairie grass background. When the coyote passed, the rabbit bounded across the open ground with unbelievably long leaps until a final lunge hurtled him back into the tall grass.

At the corral, Jim unsaddled Dancer and let him roll in the dust. He smiled with pleasure as the pony rolled all the way over. When Dancer arose, Jim curried and brushed him until his coat gleamed. Then he led the horse to the river and let him drink his fill before taking him back to the corral.

Watching through the cookshack window, Frisco observed Jim's treatment of Dancer and nodded approvingly.

# 5

"Take that lonely biscuit and mop the larrup off your plate, Jim," Frisco said, as they were finishing a big breakfast.

"Thanks," Jim answered, taking the biscuit and wiping his plate clean of molasses. "Finally, I came out even. First, there was the biscuit that needed larrup; then I had to have more larrup for the half-biscuit that was left, but your hand shook and I got too much larrup. I guess I've downed half the larrup and biscuits in Texas."

"You can use 'em; you still look kinda puny to me."

"That's what I figured. You've been spoon-feeding me for three days. I'm beholden to you, but it's high time I was getting out on my own."

48

"You've got more spunk than good sense. Texas is mighty big, and it's a long way between spreads. I don't have to tell you that the pickin's are mighty slim out on the prairie."

"The pickings won't be any better tomorrow — or next week. I sure appreciate your hospitality, but my mind's made up. I'm pulling out right now."

"Tom Peters might put you on. You ought to wait."

"I can't wait. I'm too anxious to find out — one way or the other. Where'll I find him; out at the holding spot?"

"They'll be there," Frisco said. "I'll be joinin' them day after tomorrow. Shore hope I see you there, Jim."

"Me, too. Will you point me in the right direction as soon as I saddle Andy?"

Jim arrived at the box canyon just before noon. He approached from downwind and dismounted before nearing the cook's fire.

"Howdy," he said to a man who was kneeling by the open fire.

The cowboy-cook painfully straightened out in sections — like a carpenter's folding rule. He was wearing spurs and wide-flapped leather chaps to let the world know that he was a cowhand — not a cook. He wiped his right hand on the seat of his pants and then extended it toward Jim.

"Ah'm Moose Jackson," he said. "Wrangler for this outfit when the cook's where he oughta be."

"Howdy, Moose," Jim said, shaking his hand.

Moose was barely five feet tall in his high-heeled boots, and he weighed about 120 pounds, fully dressed — wearing batwing chaps and what must have been the highest crowned sombrero in Texas. He wore the most magnificent red handlebar moustache Jim had ever seen. Like the longhorns, who apparently used up most of their growing power on their horns, Moose appeared to have used his up on that luxuriant red moustache.

"My name's Jim Ryan."

"Yo're just in time for chow, Jim. I was just about to call the boys in," Moose said. And with that, he bellowed a call that rolled through the canyon like the challenge of a bull moose.

Jim wondered that the cattle did not stampede. A few minutes later, riders came thundering into camp from all directions. They raced in as though each man had wagered a month's wages that he could beat the rest of the boys to the chuck wagon. They pulled up at the picket line, secured their horses, loosened their cinches, and put nosebags on their animals before coming in to feed themselves.

They came in assorted sizes and shapes, these riders of the Tepee brand. Long and short; slim and broad. Seen from a distance, they were similar only in the way they walked — with cranelike hobbling gaits. The men had ridden in as though each was a part of his horse. Dismounting was like an amputation. They were like large birds that are beautiful in flight and clumsy on the ground. Jim noted their awkwardness on foot, but he felt only admiration for them.

After taking care of their mounts, the cowboys walked directly to the chuck wagon and lined up at the lowered tail gate which was used as a serving table. The back of the short, four-wheeled wagon was pigeonholed into shelves and drawers for storing the necessities of trail cooking. Beneath the bed of the wagon swung a hammocklike, dried cowhide cooney for carrying firewood or "chips."

Moose Jackson had made it clear that he was not a cook and that he did not aspire to become one, but true to the cowboy code of staying on an assigned job, he was doing his level best for the hungry men who depended on him.

Although he was cooking against his wishes and on a temporary basis, it was apparent that Moose ruled his domain with an iron hand. The men had boisterously approached the camp, but they had calmed down as they entered an imaginary circle whose radius was about fifty feet from the cook-fire. They spoke softly and walked carefully from downwind, lifting their feet high with each step to avoid kicking up any dust.

Moose filled their plates from his pot, skillet, and Dutch oven, heaping them with generous servings of son-of-a-gun stew, sowbelly and corn bread. The ever-present larrup was there to sweeten the corn bread and cowboy coffee — a coffee substitute made of parched corn.

After the working hands had been served, Moose waved Jim forward with his big iron spoon and filled a plate and cup for him.

"Still ridin' the chow-line trail?"

Recognizing the contempt-filled voice, Jim whirled and faced Curly, who had just come up behind him. His face flushed as he stood there for an indecisive moment, holding a cup in one hand and a plate in the other. He was angry and embarrassed. His anger increased as he watched the sneering grin spread over Curly's face. He turned away to set his utensils back on the tail gate.

"Jim's not riding the chow line," said Tom Peters, who had come in late with Curly. "What's more, I don't want anyone to be insulted for eating Tepee chow. A hungry man is always welcome here as my guest, and he'll be treated that way by every man who works for me."

For the second time, Tom Peters broke up an argument between Curly and Jim before they could become seriously embroiled. Looking at the angry cowboy, Jim knew that Curly would like nothing better than a chance to settle their differences right then and there. He was also getting mighty tired of being insulted. He doubted that he could whip Curly, but he would rather take a beating than endure the man's bullying.

Tom Peters picked up Jim's cup and plate and handed them to him. Then he had Moose fill his.

"Come over here, Jim," he said, walking to the far side of the chuck wagon. "I want to have a little talk with you."

That took the initiative out of Jim's hands. He followed the rancher and hunkered down beside him silently. Both of them ate, Jim wondering what the man had to say, but not wanting to come right out and ask him. He figured that his chance of joining the Tepee outfit was slim. Not only were his youth and inexperience handicaps, but Tom Peters — or any other rancher — would be unlikely to hire a tenderfoot whose conflict with an experienced hand was certain to cause trouble.

When he had finished eating, Tom Peters leaned back against the chuck wagon wheel and rolled a cigarette. "How are you feeling, Jim?" he asked.

"Couldn't be better, Mr. Peters. Thanks to Frisco's chow, I got my strength back in a hurry. He wouldn't let me give him a hand, so I came out here to ask you again for a job."

"You've got one."

"What?"

Tom Peters laughed. "Frisco thinks a lot of you and so does Ace. You've been a Tepee man since the day you bogged that steer."

"Thanks, Mr. Peters. Thanks very much," Jim said.

"You may thank me out of the other side of your mouth before the week's out. This is a rugged life, even for an experienced man. Your ignorance of ranching will make the work much harder for you. You'll start out as an all-around handy man, Jim. Make yourself useful to Frisco and Moose, and keep your eyes and ears open while you work. You can learn a lot from those two hombres."

Tom Peters walked away, leaving Jim to wonder at his unexpected good fortune. He was just a flunky, but he belonged to a good outfit. That was the important thing.

He picked up his utensils and walked to the tail gate, "Thanks for a fine meal, Moose," he said.

A smile lifted Moose's impressive red moustache, revealing his large, white teeth. "Don't mention it, Jim. Glad to have you with us."

"I just got the word that I'm not a guest any longer. The boss put me on. He told me to make myself useful to you and Frisco. What shall I do first?"

Jim did not have to ask again. He washed dishes, scrubbed pots and pans, rustled wood, greased the chuck wagon's axles, soaped and repaired harness, shod horses, and accomplished a score of other tasks around camp for the next two days. Working from dawn until after dark, he did everything that he was told to do, and he assigned himself many other jobs which he thought would help to get the outfit ready to hit the trail north toward Abilene. No job was too menial for Jim. Everything that had to be done was part of ranching — and ranching was what he wanted to do.

During his brief rest periods, Jim asked questions. Moose answered with patience, jocularity, or irritability, depending upon the nature of the question, the condition under which it was asked, the state of the fiery little man's temper, and many other unpredictables.

Frisco arrived at the holding spot on the morning of the third day, driving a buckboard full of provisions.

"So you sold the Old Man a bill of goods," he said with a friendly smile. "Glad you made it."

"Thanks to you and Ace Dawson. You two fixed it so I didn't even have to do my own talking. I'll be your flunky now that you're taking over here."

"No, you'll help Moose with the wranglin'. Runnin'

the chuck wagon's a one-man job. We won't be strangers, though. The remuda sticks pretty close to the chuck wagon on a drive. We'll see a lot of each other, Jim."

While Jim unloaded the buckboard, Frisco carefully reloaded the chuck wagon. He made sure that the water barrel was full of fresh water and free from leaks. Then he checked the chuck box shelves and drawers, which contained food and utensils. There was a chest full of odds and ends, including a good supply of rawhide strips and haywire, to be used for the repair of just about anything that might get damaged during the trail drive. Ammunition, rope, hobbles, and a score of other things that would be useful were carried in the chest.

Frisco had loaded everything needed to feed the men for more than a month and saved enough space to pack bedrolls and extra clothing that the cowboys could not carry on their saddle horses.

Frisco's last act was to check the cooney to make sure it was full of dry fuel. "We'll be using buffalo chips and cow chips before the drive is over," he predicted, "but it pays to carry all the wood we can."

The roundup was complete. The mavericks had been branded and the selected steers cut out of the gather to make up the trail herd. They would depart the following day. Jim had never been so excited as he was at the prospect of this great adventure.

"Frisco wants you to use his string, Jim," Moose told him as they rounded up the remuda that day. "He said that you'd treat 'em right."

"That's wonderful! I'll get to ride Dancer."

"Your mule is gonna be a big help," Moose continued. "The ponies stick close to him. I'd like to bell him at night, if you don't mind."

"It's all the same to me, if Andy'll put up with it," Jim said. "He usually goes along with any reasonable idea. Better let me strap it on him. He trusts me."

There were sixty-three horses in the remuda. In addition, each man had a mount which he was either riding or holding ready for emergency. The night horses were picketed nearby, where they could graze and rest until their riders were ready to saddle them for night guard.

"How many hands are going on the drive, Moose?" Jim asked.

"Six drovers, plus the Old Man, Curly, Frisco, and us two — one cowhand for every two-hundred head of cattle. "

"What makes Curly different from the rest of the hands?" Jim asked, noting the exception Moose had made.

"He's *segundo* — the number-two man in this outfit."

That was depressing news. Jim dreaded the prospect of having to take orders from him, but he was determined to earn his place on the Tepee spread. If, in order to make good, he had to swallow his pride and take whatever punishment Curly chose to inflict, he would do so. He owed that much to Frisco and Ace for having recommended him to Tom Peters.

"What's the trouble?" Moose asked. "You look like you'd et a bug."

Jim laughed. "Nothing's wrong — I'm just worked

up about the drive. I've got to get busy."

"Go back to camp and give Frisco a hand. If you can't do anything for him, crawl into yore hot roll for a couple hours. You'll be night-hawking tonight."

"What time'll I take over the remuda?"

"I'll roust you out when the time comes. From now on, nobody'll get more'n a couple hours sleep at a stretch, so get the custom of grabbin' shut-eye when you can. Sometimes that'll be while yo're forkin' a hoss."

"You really like that Texas jackrabbit, don't you, Jim?" Moose asked as Jim saddled his mule.

"I sure do. Andy and me's put in a lot of years together, and he's never once let me down. Not once! That's about all a man can ask of a friend."

"That's about all, Jim," Moose agreed.

As Andy bore him toward camp at a fast, smooth walk, Jim felt a sense of well-being that he had not known since his early boyhood — before the war had shattered the good life he had known.

"How's wranglin', Jim?" Frisco asked, as Jim dismounted and loosened Andy's cinch.

"Ask me tomorrow morning; tonight I'll be night-hawking for the first time. I guess I'll make the grade if Andy keeps them interested and Dancer takes over anytime I get into trouble. I sure appreciate your letting me use your string — especially Dancer."

"You'll make out fine — you three," Frisco said.

Everything in Frisco's domain looked neat, well organized, and complete, as though he was ready to move out or to serve a good meal on ten minutes' notice.

"What needs doing, Frisco?" Jim asked. "Need more wood or water?"

"No room for either, Jim. You'd best catch some sleep. It'll be a long night."

Since he would not be needing Andy for a while, Jim unsaddled him and was about to turn him loose.

"Better stake that critter out, Jim," Frisco advised.

"He won't run away."

"It's the custom in camp. It's best not to make exceptions."

Jim rope-staked Andy where the grass was good, before he unrolled his poncho and spread his blankets. Using his saddle for a pillow, Jim stretched out on the ground, shaded his eyes with his battered old hat, and quickly fell asleep.

The ground shook as thundering hoofbeats awakened Jim. Before he could orient himself, the air above his face was filled with flying, iron-shod hoofs. Terrified, he buried his head under the saddle yelling, "Stampede!"

Laughter mocked the cowering boy as the sound of hoofbeats faded in the distance.

Furious and ashamed, Jim threw off his blanket and leaped to his feet. Curly stood beside his horse about two hundred feet away from Jim, grinning maliciously. This was too much! He had taken all he could stand from Curly. It was time for a showdown.

Jim walked rapidly toward Curly, clenching his fists and never taking his eyes from the face he had come to hate. He was so angry that he felt sick to his stomach. Only a fight would bring relief.

58

But as he walked the long distance which the cowboy had covered before stopping his horse, Jim had time to reconsider — to remember that this man was second in command of the trail crew and that Curly could fire him. As he fought for self control, the temptation to lash out at that leering face was overpowering, but he realized that he must resist it. He unclenched his fists, took a final long look at the mocking cowboy, turned, and walked back to his bedroll.

Curly hooted, and Jim knew that his hazing had just begun. He had allowed a bully to get the upper hand.

## THE CHALLENGE

**6**

On the eve of the drive, one rider was enough to keep the steers from drifting out of the narrow mouth of the box canyon, and another could handle the saddle animals. Ace and Moose stayed out, and the rest of the men came into camp. For the first time, Jim saw the drovers who had been out on the range for several days.

He could not have met them under worse circumstances. No one spoke to him about having backed down under Curly's hazing, but it was apparent that they all knew about it. They might befriend a tenderfoot, but not a coward.

While cleaning his rifle, feeling ashamed and miserable, Jim wondered whether Frisco would now also scorn him. He could not find out while the cook was busy getting supper ready for the hungry hands, for no man ventured into the vicinity of the chuck wagon before an invitation was clearly issued. Cow camp etiquette was rigidly enforced by short-tempered camp cooks throughout the cattle country.

The hands were bunched together, waiting for Frisco's call. Jim had no idea what they were talking about, but he longed to be one of them. Although he was working for Tom Peters, Jim knew that he was neither a guest nor one of the bunch. Although he was accustomed to being alone, he had never felt so lonely as he did in this camp among strangers who did not want his company.

Suddenly, he got angry. Jim wanted to keep his new job, but not as a pariah. It was time for a showdown. Walking toward the group, he hoped for the best but was prepared for the worst. Whether they approved or not, he had been hired to ride with the Tepee men, and he was going to be at home wherever that brand was seen.

As he drew near, the easy talk of the men slacked off until there was silence. Jim stopped at the edge of the gathering and hopefully waited for a friendly greeting.

Curly looked at the mountain boy, staring contemptuously, first at Jim and then at his rifle.

"A Tennessee hillbilly, a broken-down mule, and a flintlock rifle," he drawled with a sardonic grin. "Tom Peters sure is takin' on the dregs this season. He can't help takin' in a dogie, no matter how useless it is."

Jim's ears burned, but he said nothing as he stared at a clump of mesquite in the distance.

"Reckon you'll ever amount to anythin', clodhopper?"

Jim continued to stare over Curly's shoulder, maintaining his silence.

"It appears to me, you're just another plow-chasin' gutless wonder. Bet you couldn't hit the broadside of a barn from the inside with that old blunderbuss."

Observing a coyote lurking at the edge of the distant mesquite, Jim estimated the range and wind effect and calculated the carrying power of the load in his rifle. It would be a long shot and a very difficult one in the fading light of dusk. He hesitated.

"Maybe I just oughta take that musket before you hurt yourself with it, sonny," Curly said, as he slowly rose to his feet.

Swiftly, Jim snapped the rifle to his shoulder, pointing it in Curly's direction. The cowboy dropped to the ground as the rifle roared, filling the air with black, pungent smoke. Reloading as he ran, Jim leaped over the prostrate cowboy and dashed to the clump of mesquite before the other man could rise or speak.

He returned with the dead coyote as Curly pulled his pistol and started after him.

The *segundo* stopped, stared at the coyote with disbelief. Then, enraged by Jim's humiliating action, he holstered his Colt and strode toward him with his big fists doubled, his eyes blazing.

Jim decided to take the offensive rather than wait for the cowboy to start dusting his hide. He threw the coyote carcass at the angry man's feet, stopping him in his tracks.

"You're wearing a shiny Colt on your hip," he said. "Let's see how good you are with it."

"With you aimin' that cocked rifle at me?"

"I ain't challenging you to a gunfight. I answered your question about my rifle. Now I'm asking if you can hit the broadside of a barn from the inside with your pistol, or is it just a pretty doodad you wear to impress women and small children?"

Curly's face was livid, but he had to control his anger and accept Jim's challenge. The other hands had been impressed by his marksmanship, and now Curly had to perform with equal skill. Nothing less would do.

He could not make a long shot with the pistol. Its accuracy was limited to about twenty-five yards, and he was not too sure of himself at that range.

One of the hands took over when Curly hesitated. He picked up a chunk of wood that had been brought in for fuel.

"Okay, Curly?" he asked.

The cowboy quickly regained his composure. This was his specialty. "A little farther back," he answered.

"We don't have much use for your kind of shootin', kid," he said. "Out here a man packs a weapon that's good at close range, handy to carry, and quick to draw."

He nodded at the cowboy, who then tossed the chunk of wood high into the air. Curly fired, and there was a cheer from the men as the target jerked in midair.

Almost simultaneously, something flashed in the light of the setting sun, and the target was knocked off course. It hit the ground with a knife buried in it.

Jim walked over to the stick and brought it back to the group. He pulled the knife out only when he was sure that they all could see that it was centered in the target and deeply buried in it. Since it had been necessary for him to show off his skill, he wanted to make full use of the incident to improve his standing with the men.

He had bested Curly dramatically, but he knew that he had pressed his luck as far as he dared. He turned away and walked over to Andy before Curly could involve him in another test.

He brushed the mule's back, carefully spread the saddle blanket on him, and then saddled and bridled him. He had no intention of leaving until he had eaten, but he did not want to stay in the vicinity of the angry *segundo*. If possible, it would be best to postpone the fight that was sure to come, until he could make himself useful to Tom Peters.

"Come and get it before I throw it to the coyotes — what's left of 'em, that is," Frisco amended his customary chow call with this comment on Jim's marksmanship.

As the hands lined up at the chuck wagon, Jim made it a point to be the last in line. Frisco winked as he filled Jim's plate and gave him an extra sourdough biscuit. He said nothing, but the reassuring wink made Jim's spirits soar.

A covert glance at Curly during the meal confirmed Jim's belief that his momentary victory had increased the *segundo's* animosity. There would be more trouble between the two of them. Jim was really sorry about that, but he would never back down again. He finished his meal, put his utensils into the wreck pan, and thanked Frisco for a good bait.

"Yo're the thankin'est feller I ever met," Frisco said. "This chow's part of your pay now, so you don't have to thank me for it."

"I've got a lot to thank you for, Frisco; I reckon I'll be thanking you to my dying day," Jim said. "And I hope I'll still be eating your sourdough biscuits when that day comes."

Jim rode out to the remuda to relieve Moose.

"Frisco's got the chuck wagon operating," he said. "Better get there and wolf a bait before he throws it out."

Moose stroked his impressive moustache as he grinned at Jim. "Yo're feelin' real chipper, young 'un. What's got into you?"

"I've got a lot to feel chipper about, Moose: a good job with a top outfit, the use of Frisco's string, and I'm full to the gills with steak and sourdough biscuits. I'm sitting on top of the world."

"Wait'll you've et Texas dust for a couple of hundred miles and nursed this cavvy through a thunderstorm and helped pull the chuck wagon across the Red River. Then tell me all about the glory and happiness to be found on a cattle drive."

"Moose, you're a killjoy. Why don't you go on in and eat before you talk me into quitting this job?"

"I'll be back before mornin', Jim. Take it easy and remember everything I've learned you."

Jim transferred his saddle from Andy to Dancer. He smiled as the mule ignored the band of horses, taking it as a matter of course when they flocked around him.

"Your head was way too big before we came to Texas," Jim told him, "and now they're spoiling you rotten. You think you're something pretty special."

Andy flapped a hairy ear as Jim mounted. Given free rein, Dancer began slowly to circle the remuda without guidance from his rider. Jim settled back in the saddle and relaxed while he observed the band.

He did not feel that the Kentucky flintlock was out of place on his pommel. Later, when he had earned enough money and got a chance to go to town, he would buy the right clothes, a good rope, saddle, bridle, spurs, and a pistol. Meanwhile, he would get along with what he had and not worry about what anybody thought.

Herding the remuda was easy that night. Being near camp where there was good grazing and plenty of water, the horses had no desire to leave the valley. From the way they kept Andy in sight at all times, Jim knew that they would not wander away. But he kept watch over them as though they were apt to spook at any moment. He was taking no chances on losing his job before he really got started on it.

After dark, he heard a distant cowboy singing to the cattle, lulling the herd as he circled them. His song was only slightly more melodious than the wailing of the nearby coyote that greeted the rising moon with a weird howl. Jim had heard coyotes howl every night since he came West. It was a night sound which never failed to haunt him.

Moonlight washed the Texas landscape with a silver

brightness. The moon appeared larger than he had ever seen it before as it rose skyward from the plain.

The strains of a new song from the night herder brought Jim's thoughts back to the task at hand. Dancer continued to circle the cavvy at a steady walk, never stumbling on the rough ground and never making a sudden movement which might startle the spookier horses. Jim appreciatively patted the neck of his capable mount.

Time passed quickly that night. Jim was surprised when Moose appeared. The cowboy was singing as he approached the cavvy, so he would not startle either the horses or their nighthawk.

"Howdy, Jim. Still got most of the ponies you started out with?"

"I think so, give or take twenty or thirty."

"Then catch a little sleep. I'll hold 'em until mornin'."

"I'm too excited to sleep, Moose. How about letting me ride with you for an hour or so?"

"Good enough," the cowboy agreed genially.

"Let me unsaddle Dancer. No sense in keeping him on the go just because I don't feel like sleeping. I'll meet you on the next go-round, Moose."

Unsaddled, Dancer kicked his heels high as though ridding himself of the responsibilities he had borne. Then he trotted away and joined the other ponies.

Jim's whistle brought Andy to him. He was about to mount with neither saddle nor bridle, but he saw that the horses were getting restive because he had moved the mule away from them. That would defeat the purpose of the nighthawks — to give the animals a chance to rest and graze before a hard day's work. He dismounted and shook out his lariat. Selecting a handsome sorrel with white-stockinged forelegs, he trailed his loop, approached slowly. With an easy toss, he caught the horse with his first cast.

Jim approached the sorrel with his bridle in hand.

"Better turn him loose and dab yore loop on another one, Jim," Moose said as he came near.

"What's the matter with this one?"

"He's a top-hand horse."

"Meaning?"

"He's one of Curly's string. The top hand in any outfit gets his pick of the ponies and nobody else rides 'em. Matter of fact, Jim, you'd better get to know which ponies are Frisco's. He said you could use his string."

"Obliged, Moose," Jim said as he freed the sorrel. "I don't want to offend anybody, and I sure don't want to rile Curly."

He selected a small black from Frisco's string, saddled it, and joined Moose on his next round.

"I hear you had a run-in with Curly," Moose said.

"Nothing serious," Jim replied. "I ain't seekin' trouble with him, and he sure can't prove anything by whipping me — I've got no reputation around here — so I guess it's about petered out."

"You admit he could whip you?"

"Sure, any day in the week and twice on Sundays. He's older, bigger, stronger, and probably done lots of fighting. I don't claim to be the world's best scrapper.

In fact, I'm a peace-loving citizen from way back."

"That sure beats me," Moose said, shaking his head. "I heard you stood right up to him like you wasn't afraid."

"I'm not afraid. I don't think I can beat him, but I'm not afraid of taking a beating."

"He's whipped every man in this outfit, save two. Frisco's no challenge, now that he's all beat-up, and Tom Peters is the boss, so there'd be no point in Curly takin' him on. But everybody else has taken his beatin' from Curly."

"Why does Mr. Peters put up with him? Are good men that hard to come by?"

"The Old Man don't interfere with fights and the like. That's the way the boys want it. Besides, Curly's top hand. He's good to have around when the goin' gets rough. I can't say I like him much, but I'm glad he's in our outfit."

"Back where I come from, he'd be put down as a bully and nobody'd want him around, anymore than they'd want a mean dog in the neighborhood."

"Suppose the mean dog was the best coon dog in the county. Would you run him out?"

Jim grinned, "Well, if you want to compare an ornery cowboy with a good hunting dog . . ."

"Don't take it too humorous, Jim," Moose warned. "Curly's a hard case, and he don't care how he mangles a man. Tangle with him and you'll know you've been in something more brutal than a schoolyard fist fight."

"I still don't think I have to mix it up with him. I've no ambition to conquer Curly."

"You conquered him in a couple of departments already, and you can believe me when I say he won't let it lay there."

"I'll be careful, Moose. If we fight, it'll be him who starts it — I guarantee you that."

Jim rode with Moose through the rest of the night, taking advantage of the opportunity to pump all the information he could from the little wrangler, who happened to be in a talkative mood. As dawn took over the job of lighting the plains from a waning moon, they rounded up the saddle horses and headed toward camp.

When the remuda came into sight, the cowboys formed a large circle, acting as human fenceposts, stretching their lariats from man to man until a rope-and-man corral had been made, with a wide opening facing the oncoming horses.

"Head Andy in there, and the ponies'll follow," Moose bellowed, and in a few moments the herd entered and the men closed the opening.

Curly was the roper. He entered the rope corral with his lariat trailing a large loop.

"Midnight," Ace Dawson called.

Curly approached a big black gelding. The loop shot out with the accuracy of a striking snake, settling around Midnight's neck. Ace led his horse out of the enclosure, bridled it, and then rejoined the others to maintain the rope corral, while the rest of the animals were being selected and caught.

Curly never missed. Unerringly, he roped each animal named or described by its user. In just a few minutes, all of the horses needed for the first leg of the day's drive had been cut out of the band, and Moose and Jim returned the remaining horses to their range.

Moose sent Jim in to eat breakfast, with instructions to relieve him as soon as he finished eating. Jim may have been too excited to sleep, but he was not going to have any trouble taking in food. Of that he was sure.

Frisco greeted him with a warm smile. "How'd you and Andy make out?"

"Andy really shines!" Jim said. "He takes to cowboying like he was born in Texas. Those cow ponies follow him like a flock of sheep. They listen to everything he says. Knowing Andy like I do, I'll bet he's telling 'em nothing but a pack of lies."

"And yourself?"

"I just sat on Dancer's back, like a crow on a high branch, and watched the world go by. There's no problem when you give that little bay his head. He's a fine animal, Frisco, and that's for sure."

"For them kind words, you get an extra spoon of larrup and a double helping of sourdough biscuits," said the cook, as he heaped Jim's plate high with good food: four biscuits, a big steak, a heap of pinto beans, and a cup of cowboy coffee to wash it all down.

"Lucky I'm not very hungry," Jim commented dryly. "This piddlin' meal would hardly keep a hungry man alive — for more'n six or eight weeks."

"If you can't eat it, leave it, and the next time I'll halve it."

"Oh, I'll eat it all. I've been told it's considered bad

manners to leave chow on your plate, and I sure don't propose to insult the man who feeds me."

He ate the steak and beans, mopped up the larrup with his last biscuit, and drank the last drop of coffee in his cup before dropping his dishes in the wreck pan.

"That was real good, Frisco," he said. "I think it'll hold me until noontime rolls around."

"I haven't seen eatin' like that since the time a bear got into my larrup back in the spring of '66," Frisco said admiringly. "You eat like you was sure of gettin' lockjaw tomorrow."

"Sorry to make a pig of myself," Jim said. "I want to go back and watch the drive start."

"Don't be sorry. I admire watchin' an eater like you, Jim. See you when we make our nooning."

Jim tightened the cinch on his saddle and mounted.

"Moose'll be here in a few minutes," he said.

"His steak's in the pan," Frisco answered.

Jim covered the short distance to the remuda at an easy gallop.

"Why don't you ride up on that rise?" Moose asked, sensing Jim's excitement. "You can see everything from the back of your horse up there. The remuda won't need much looking after with Andy around."

"Thanks, Moose." Jim did not have to be urged. He rode to the hillock, checked the remuda, and found all of the animals bunched within a few yards of Andy. The comfort-loving mule was not about to leave good grass and water for some unknown destination without being persuaded to do so.

Jim looked out across the box canyon and saw that the longhorns were still in their holding spot. The cowboys were just beginning to move them toward the canyon's only exit. Things were starting slowly as the riders scoured the brush, gathering cattle which had strayed from the main herd. As yet, they had not moved any longhorns out of the canyon.

So much was happening so smoothly that Jim could see little progress at first. He sought out the big white-stockinged sorrel and watched that horse and its rider attentively, realizing that Curly was the man to watch for the exciting action that was about to begin.

# 7

Curly worked with quiet patience as he drove a big red steer out of the brush toward the mouth of the canyon. Jim felt a grudging respect for the *segundo* as he watched him apply just enough pressure on the steer to keep him moving in the right direction without making him attack or bolt for freedom.

There was no yelling or rope-popping at this time. All of the drovers moved like mounted ghosts in the gray dawn, quietly urging other steers to follow their big red leader out of the box canyon and allowing them to graze as they went.

As the forward motion became more pronounced, three or four other rangy longhorns began to vie for leadership and others sought preferred traveling positions in the herd. Jim sensed that a few feisty steers could cause a lot of trouble at this stage of the drive.

The cowboys spotted potential troublemakers and expertly cut them out before they could create a disturbance. All a steer had to do was bellow, roll his eyes, or tail-up, and a drover would ride up and separate him from the other longhorns until he calmed down.

Now the leaders were walking faster. Curly and Ace Dawson flanked them as they worked their way out through the canyon mouth. Then Curly veered to the right, and Ace gradually turned toward him, swinging the head of the herd northward. Responding to the subtle guidance of the experienced drovers working with well-trained cow ponies, the herd headed out for Abilene.

The steers settled into their traveling positions, and the drive began. Ace and Curly rode point, abreast of the lead steers, and other drovers followed them at intervals of about two hundred and fifty yards riding swing. They did not haze the animals, just applied enough pressure to contain them within rough limits. When a ringy longhorn decided to take to the brush, a flank rider would drive him back into line.

The herd began to take shape as Ace and Curly stepped up the pace of the leaders and the tail riders brought up the last of the steers out of the box canyon. The herd strung out to a length of about a mile and a half. Jim estimated its average width at about a hundred and fifty yards, although it was much narrower in some places and a little wider in others.

Jim left his vantage point and brought the remuda into position behind the herd, far enough back to avoid the cloud of dust raised by almost five thousand hoofs, but close enough so he could quickly give a fresh mount to any rider who might have to change horses in a hurry.

Soon after Jim brought the remuda into line, Frisco drove up behind him, circled the band, and pulled in ahead of the remuda. Moose, who had been helping Frisco break camp, pulled up alongside Jim.

"You've got yourself a real critter there," Moose bellowed. "That old mule steps out like my old troop commander, and the ponies follow as pretty as you please."

"I was just thinking the same thing. Andy acts like he was born for this job. He takes to Texas like it was a big bag of oats."

"There'll be no problems here, Jim," Moose said, "why don't you ride up the line and see what the boys are doin'?"

"Thanks. I'd like that."

Not wanting to run afoul of the surly *segundo,* Jim rode up the left flank of the herd, staying well out to avoid spooking any skittish longhorns.

There had been only three cows on the farm Jim's father had owned back in Tennessee, three white-faced milk cows that spent all day browsing or chewing their cuds. Never ornery, always placid, they were thoroughly domesticated. Jim never passed a farm animal without saying a couple of words and patting it reassuringly.

All of the money in the state of Texas would not have induced Jim to dismount and attempt to pat any longhorn in this herd. Lean, rangy, and fearsomely horned, they were not pets of any man. In the Texas cattle country, men would never try to herd cattle afoot as eastern farm boys did. Out here a dismounted cowboy was as wary of an approaching longhorn as he would be of a grizzly bear or a buffalo.

Jim passed up the drag and swing riders on the left flank. He was anxious to meet Ace Dawson again. Now the point rider was positioned to the left and a few yards to the rear of the lead steer, allowing the red long-horn to lead without harrassment. Jim stayed behind where he could observe the cowboy in action for a couple of miles before coming up to join him.

The herd was traveling at a faster pace than he had expected. These long-legged beeves were capable of walking an ordinary steer to death in a day, if there was any way to make such an animal try to keep up with them. Jim knew that the object of the drive was to take a herd of half-wild cattle from a land where there were too many cattle and too few dollars to a market where there was too little meat and a lot of money to pay for it.

A five-dollar steer from Texas could sell for fifty dol-lars in Kansas. Cattlemen from the Lone Star State could drive herds north and sell them to anxious buyers and become wealthy in a hurry — if they finished the drive with most of their cattle, and if the longhorns arrived in good condition.

It seemed to Jim that they should slow down and give the cattle opportunity to eat good grass, drink enough water, and get enough rest so they would weigh at least as much, or preferably more, when they arrived as when they started. They could not do that if they continued to travel at this pace; even a tenderfoot could see that.

There was a lot of coordination in the drive, but some of it became apparent only after Jim had studied the actions of the two point men and their horses — and even of the big red lead steer.

The men rode as a team without exchanging visible or audible signals. A turn toward the left was accomplished by Curly crowding in toward the lead longhorn while Ace drifted away from him. Big Red veered away from the oncoming Curly toward the space left open by Ace. The other steers held their relative positions, except for a few potential troublemakers that were still trying to get into occupied positions which they coveted for reasons known only to themselves.

When rebellious steers tried to break away from their places in the undulating line, Curly and Ace permitted them some latitude so long as they did not disturb other beeves. When trouble threatened, the two drovers reacted quickly to forestall it. They went into action, this cowboy-cow pony team, with quick, smooth efficiency. Without waiting for direction by their riders, the cow ponies would close in on an unruly longhorn and, evading the feints of long, sharp horns, block his path no matter which way he tried to dodge and guide him back into line while the rider flicked the "bitter-end" of his rope near the steer's face to help urge him along.

As the drive progressed, the restive steers became more discouraged and most of them held their places in line. But there was one obstreperous old mossyhorn on Curly's flank that continued to break away. He was giving the *segundo* a bad time and making other steers more and more restless. Even Jim could see that this ornery steer would cause a lot of trouble unless he was stopped in a hurry. Three times, the longhorn broke away and charged toward the dense, shoulder-high brush, and each time Curly chased him back into line. But every time he broke away he caused more nervousness among the other steers, and each time he was harder to catch and run back. He had to be stopped.

Curly was not a patient man at best, and it was apparent that he had passed his boiling point. He and that longhorn were going to tangle pronto. Jim had no idea of what more the cowboy could do to discourage the steer. He was so angry that Jim knew he would shoot the animal if it were not for the likelihood that the entire herd would stampede at the sound of a shot.

"Howdy, partner."

Jim was startled by Ace's greeting, not having realized that the drover had dropped back to greet him.

"Howdy, Ace. Been meaning to thank you for putting in a good word for me. It helped me to get my job."

"Don't mention it, Jim. I just told the Old Man what I saw. That's an outrider's job: findin', fixin', and reportin'."

"I really appreciate it. You gave me a hand when I needed it most."

"How're you makin' out, Jim? Got the remuda in good shape?"

"Moose's got 'em in tow right now. He sent me up to learn what I can about driving cattle."

"Any bafflements?"

"Not more'n a couple hundred that I can think of right off. One thing that beats me is why we're movin' so fast. I thought the idea was to keep the meat on these critters, but the way we're going, we're gonna walk the tallow right off 'em. As it is, there's not enough tallow on this whole herd to make one good candle."

"We push 'em hard the first few days to get 'em away from familiar ground and into strange territory where they won't be so apt to run off. We want to get 'em so tired they won't have enough energy to spook the first couple of nights out."

Just then the old mossyhorn cut out again and ran toward the brush, and three other steers got big ideas and took off after him.

"Curly's had a bellyful of that steer. He's gonna tail him, sure as sin."

The raging steer raced out of the herd with eyes rolling wildly, hooking his great span of horns from side to side. Then he lowered his head and dashed toward the mesquite thicket, with the other three rebels right behind him.

Curly roweled his mount and bore down on the steer like a man possessed. The fine horse outran the long-legged steer, closing in as though he knew exactly what Curly planned to do.

As he came up behind the mossyhorn steer, Curly grabbed its erect tail, spurred his horse, and heaved.

The longhorn somersaulted and hit the ground with a jolting thud. He grunted and lay outstretched for a moment. Curly rode around the dazed animal, ready to repeat the dosage, if necessary, but the steer staggered to his feet, shook his head, and then docilely trotted back to his position in the herd. The other three steers, having lost their leader, ran back to the herd as Curly flicked the honda of his lariat at them.

"That's a pretty rough way to treat an animal," Jim growled disgustedly.

"Tailin' ain't gentle," Ace agreed, "but it was either that or shoot the critter. He would have caused more trouble, day and night, until he finally started a stampede. This ain't an easy life for man nor beast, but I doubt that you'll find one hand in a hundred who's harder on livestock than he has to be. You'll see plenty of rough stuff on the drive, but you'll also see the other side, if you look for it."

Jim believed Ace, but he did not like the idea of abusing an animal for any reason. Maybe he would have been less critical about it if another cowboy had done the tailing, but he had put Curly down as a mean man.

The punished steer now held his position as though nothing less than a Texas twister could drive him out of his place in line. He was a thoroughly convinced animal.

"Are they always that meek after a tailing?" Jim asked.

"No. Some lay down and won't get up again unless you flog 'em with a lariat or build a fire between their legs. Some just won't get up, and you have to put a bullet where it'll do the most good and leave 'em for coyote bait. It might take a couple of tailings to do the job on others. Like people, there's no two longhorns exactly alike, and you can't tell what one of 'em will do. I can tell you, though, that we'll get to know some of these ringy old mossyhorns like they was our children before we get this herd to Abilene.

"There'll be leaders, followers, troublemakers — like our beat-up friend over on Curly's flank. But the ones to really worry about are the low-lyin', ornery critters that go along meek as can be, just awaitin' for the right time to bust out with their own special brand of calamity. Maybe it'll be at a river crossin', or when a lightnin' storm breaks, or when we come up on a buffalo herd, or a band of maraudin' redskins suddenly comes out of nowhere. Whatever it is, they'll wait for the time that's best for them and worst for us and try to trigger the whole herd into a mess of devilment. And that kind's hard to spot until it's too late."

"Then you can't tell which ones are going to be most ornery?"

"That's the hitch, Jim. You can't tell for sure by the way they look or the way they act. If you could, we'd keep a special eye on 'em, or get rid of 'em the first time we needed meat for the chuck wagon. All you can do is be ready for anything and watch 'em all, all the time."

"What do you watch for?"

"Trouble keeps breakin' out for no good reason that you can figure out. Then you notice that one longhorn is always on hand where it starts, so you keep special watch on him. The trick is to keep lookin', and that means you have to travel about ten times farther and faster than the steers do, ridin' back and forth. That's why we have a big remuda; ridin' herd on these longhorns is mighty rough on cow ponies."

"I guess I'd better get back to the remuda now, Ace. See you at chow."

"*Adios,* Jim."

Jim rode far enough from the herd to avoid bothering the cattle or the men who drove them. He waved as he passed the left flanker, and the cowboy responded by touching his sombrero brim in a soft salute.

Riding drag was the worst job, Jim decided. That's where the dust was thickest and the critters the least responsive. The stragglers kept the drag riders busy every foot of the way.

Jim wanted to ride over and talk with the drag rider, but he decided that it would be better to settle for a distant observation. The cowboy had his red bandanna tied around his face to keep the dust out of his nose and mouth. Jim wondered that the man did not go blind from the dust that filled his unprotected eyes day after day.

His own eyes ached from the glare of the Texas sunshine; his throat was parched, and the sweat ran down his back in rivulets. Jim was accustomed to hard work, but not to the intense light that burned down on the open plain and the dust which penetrated his clothing and even seemed to filter through the pores of his skin.

He looked longingly at the big sombrero worn by the drag cowboy. Its wide brim shaded the man from the blazing sun, and the high crown protected his head from the heat. It was the ideal hat for this work. Jim was determined to get the right outfit as soon as he could. Not a day passed that he did not promise himself that.

The chuck wagon followed the herd just behind the dust cloud — far enough behind it for comfort — if there could be any comfort riding a springless wagon over rough country. Frisco did not mind the ride.

"How's it goin', Jim?" the cook asked.

"Just fine, Frisco. The herd's moving right along. Curly had some trouble with a ringy old mossyhorn, but he tailed him and now that critter's moseying along like a bossy cow."

"You may never get to be a real drover," Frisco said with a grin, "but you sure pick up the lingo fast."

"I'm headin' back to the remuda. Anything I can do for you first?"

"Not a thing. See you at nooning."

The remuda was not far behind the chuck wagon. Jim pulled off to the side and let the band pass him before greeting Moose, who was trailing them. The horses followed Andy eagerly, and he acted as though he had invented trailing. Jim studied each passing horse to see how many of them he could name.

"Learn anything, Jim?" Moose asked.

"Sure did. Between the two of us, I reckon you and I know everything there is to know about cattle."

"That so? Then tell me the difference between a fast brand and a slow brand, cowboy."

"That's one of the things you know, Moose."

Moose laughed good naturedly. "Yo're sure feeling yore oats, young 'un. A few weeks in the saddle's the sure cure for that."

They rode side by side for a few miles. The band needed no guidance with Andy in the lead, so Jim was able to concentrate on his horse studying. He was learning to identify them by color, bearing, size, and characteristics; the positions they held in respect to others in the band; their inclination to be frisky or lazy, nervous or calm, easy-going or irritable.

Moose helped him by naming those he was questioned about, describing their special qualities, and telling Jim which cowboys rode each of them.

"Things are going pretty well for the first day out, aren't they?"

"Smooth as silk. We're drivin' 'em at a pretty good rate, so they don't have a chance to get into much devilment, but they can't keep goin' this fast or we'll walk all the meat off 'em. It'll be different when we've been on the trail awhile, especially if there's many dry stretches."

"Is that likely this time of year?"

"You never know. Queer things happen to water out here. What was a river last year at this time might be a dry bed this year. That's one reason why the Old Man scouts the trail ahead of the herd; that and a mess of other reasons."

"For instance?"

"You'll pick up most of the for instances before we get to Abilene, Jim. Just keep yore eyes and ears open along the way."

# THE FIGHT

## 8

They traveled seventy miles the first week — seventy long, rough miles that challenged the skill and strength of men and horses. Drovers, cow ponies, and steers were now trail broken. The rate of travel had been slowed to a reasonable speed which did not run weight off the lean steers. In general, the drive moved well in spite of frequent jousts between overworked cowboys and unruly steers. Even after the drive had settled into a routine, there never was a time when the cowboys could relax their vigil.

Every morning Tom Peters left camp before sunup to scout the trail ahead, and the point riders followed his sign. The men saw little of the Old Man except at night halts, when he returned to report on the trail ahead.

The drovers changed sides at least once a day. The point riders still held the point. The flankers kept riding swing, but they shifted positions from side to side so the downwind riders would not have to eat dust all day long.

Every night the herd was thrown off the trail to graze and sleep where the grass was good, usually where there was a slight slope for the longhorns to bed down on.

Now Jim knew every horse by name and was familiar enough with their characteristics and individual traits to know which of them needed special watching and handling — which were trustworthy and which would stray away, if given a chance.

"Think you could handle the band by yourself, Jim?" Tom Peters asked one night as they sat by the fire.

Jim hesitated. He was getting along well, learning a lot, and he had not gotten into any trouble during the times Moose was away from the remuda. But he still had a lot to learn about wrangling, and there had been no real emergencies to test him yet. He wanted to accept the job but was not at all sure he was ready for it yet.

"I need Moose with the herd. He's too good a man to waste on wrangling."

Jim accepted the statement without taking offense. He knew that the wrangler held the lowest rank of all the hands on a cattle drive, and he knew that Moose was a good man.

"I reckon I can handle the remuda. I sure want to try, if you're willing to give me the chance," Jim said.

"That I am. Moose says you're doing a good job, and so does Frisco. From now on, you're drawing wrangler's wages. We're depending on you to keep the band in good condition and ready when and where we need 'em."

That evening Moose gave Jim some final advice. "Don't ride close-herd. The ponies need plenty of freedom to graze or they won't get enough to eat. Working alone, you can't watch 'em twenty-four hours a day. You'll have to hobble some of 'em at night. Bring 'em up to the rope corral every morning, and if a couple of 'em are missin', as most likely they will be more'n half the time, don't fret about it. Bring in what you have so the boys can mount up. Wait till they get the longhorns on the trail, then let the rest of the horses graze while you round up the strays. The object is to round 'em all up before nooning."

Jim was pretty sure he knew which horses would have to be hobbled at night. Some were inclined to pair off, so if he hobbled the more footloose one of each pair the other would probably not wander away. He wouldn't have to hobble Andy, and he was confident that most of the ponies would continue to stay close to his mule. But he did not intend to risk facing the hands with too few horses some morning. A cowboy afoot on a Texas cattle drive was no cowboy at all.

He decided to hobble only twelve of the horses — the youngest and spookiest and most cantankerous of the band.

There was a little pinto that shied away from every dust devil; a roan that was not yet bridle broken and that Jim had never seen Ace ride at night; a wild-eyed sorrel with a tendency to bite any horse that came up on his off side. Jim suspected that this one was going blind in his right eye, for he was upset by the approach of anything from that side. He might spook the whole band if something startled him in the night.

The horses were accustomed to Jim now. Most of them allowed him to hobble them without much resistance — he had to rope the pinto and the wild-eyed sorrel before he could buckle on their hobbles, but he managed easily. Jim was becoming adept with his lariat, thanks to Frisco's training and his enthusiastic daily practice.

But he still had not tried roping a steer from the back of a galloping horse. He knew that Tom Peters and his men would object to his practicing during the drive, so he contented himself with the kind of roping he needed as a wrangler.

He approached Andy with a set of hobbles in his hand. The reproachful look the old mule gave him was so expressive that Jim laughed aloud. "Why, you lop-eared Texas jackrabbit, I'd never hobble you, and you know it." He rubbed Andy's ears while he talked, and the mule nodded appreciatively.

"I'm depending on you to hold these scatterbrained cayuses in close, where I can find 'em in the morning," he said. "You'd better keep that irresistible charm of yours working all the time. I sure can't see what attraction you have for those cow ponies, but I'm glad you have it."

He hobbled the last horse just as the terminal light of day was fading. He took a final look around to reassure himself that all was well. He would bed down where he could be near the band, but he wanted to go back to the chuck wagon for a talk with Frisco before he turned in.

As he walked to the chuck wagon, he heard a cowboy singing to the herd. It was a hymn that Jim had heard as a small boy.

"What's the night herder singing, Frisco?" he asked.

"I don't know. I've heard it a thousand times out here on the prairie, but the men who sing those songs hardly ever know the words. They just make up their own as they go along. I guess most of 'em just sing the music they remember best and can sing the easiest."

Frisco handed Jim a huge slab of pie. "Here's something that might interest the newest wrangler in Texas."

"Nothing could interest me more. How do you find the time to run this chow cart, build three meals a day while you're on the move, and still turn out enough pies for such a big gang?"

"I'll tell you something, Jim. Like most trail cooks, I was a cowhand for a long time before I ever rode a chuck wagon, and every outfit I really liked working for put out good grub. There's times when nothing will lift a beat-down man as high as a steaming cup of coffee and a wedge of pie. In this outfit there's always a pot of hot coffee waitin' for the night guards when they come off work. Even cowboy coffee goes a long way toward making a hard job bearable on a cold or wet night."

"I can't say I ever tasted a better piece of pie."

"Pie won't come your way too often between meals, so don't get any ideas about hauntin' the chuck wagon. Mostly, when there's any left I save it for the night riders. Anybody else reaches for it at the risk of losin' a hand. And that's a fact."

Jim didn't get much sleep that night. Every time he started to doze off in the hot roll he had spread out near the band, he awakened with a start, afraid that he had overslept.

The voice of a faraway night rider soothed Jim, and the sound of Andy's bell was reassuring. The low-hanging stars fascinated him. He had seldom seen more than a few of them through the dense foliage of his Tennessee woods. The stars seemed bigger, brighter, and closer here. He was now learning how to determine direction at night by them. This had not been possible or necessary in his hill country, but it was as useful in this ocean of grass as it was on the seven seas.

He awoke before first-light, hurriedly rolled his poncho and blanket, located Dancer, and began to check his band. Andy greeted him with a shattering bray.

"Quiet, you hammerheaded mountain canary. You'll wake up the men and stampede the cattle." He patted the mule's rump. "Did you hold 'em together for me?"

Anxiously scanning the pasturage as he circled the horses, Jim was cheered by the compactness of his remuda. He found most of the animals grazing in pairs or in small bunches within earshot of Andy's bell. Only two of the animals were missing and that was as well as he and Moose had done on any previous morning during the drive. Jim had hobbled the right ponies, and now all he had to do was drive them toward camp where the men would make their rope corral.

He banded the horses into a tighter gather and then left them and rode toward camp to see whether the hands were ready for him yet. After riding a short distance, he could see the cowboys assembling near the chuck wagon. The time had come to deliver the band to the drovers.

Jim released the hobbled ponies and headed Andy toward the chuck wagon. The horses, frisky in the cold morning air, romped like colts for a few moments before trotting into line behind the mule and heading toward camp. Jim did not attempt to control them in spite of their apparent wildness. These morning romps were normal — just part of their daily routine. They were calm enough as Andy led them through the opening of the rope corral. They followed him in without hesitation.

But before the men could close their circle around the band, the wild-eyed sorrel suddenly tossed his head high and broke toward the opening, found his escape route blocked by another horse which he viciously bit on the neck. The injured pony screamed with pain and rage and both animals dashed out of the corral. Near-panic hit Jim as he saw that the excitement was spreading to other horses. He touched his heel to Dancer's flank and started to rein him into position to block the bolting horses.

Dancer responded instantly to his unspoken command, so Jim gave the cutting pony his head. The smart little animal spun around and took off at a dead run until he flanked the sorrel, then he cut in toward the unruly horse. As he did, Jim unfastened his lariat from the saddle, shook out a large loop and slowly spun it over his shoulder. The rope-wise sorrel promptly spun around and headed for the corral, followed by the other rebel, and the men closed the circle as the two animals dashed into the enclosure.

Curly stepped into the corral and began roping horses. Jim sat loose in his saddle and waited outside the corral for the selections to be completed, so he could take the remainder of the band back to pasture. After breakfast he would find the two strays while the herd was being thrown back on the trail. As Moose had taught him, he would bring all of the horses up in time for the noon halt.

The cowboys bridled their selected mounts, and all was going well until Curly's turn came.

"Where's Cutter?" he yelled at Jim. "What's happened to my sorrel?"

"He strayed," Jim replied. "I'll have him for you at noon."

"I want him right now, you fiddle-footed hillbilly. And I don't want any smart answers out of you."

Jim's anger mounted, but he controlled his temper and said nothing.

"Don't sit there like a popeyed toad," Curly roared. "Get out and find my pony. I mean right now!"

"Don't you want to take another horse in case I can't find Cutter right away?" Jim suggested.

"Get them critters out of here!" Curly waved his arms to scatter the remuda as the cowboys broke the circle.

Frightened by the flailing arms of the angry *segundo*, the horses milled about, but Andy, who had never been abused by a man, calmly stood his ground and viewed the cowboy without fear.

Curly viciously slashed the mule across the face with his heavy quirt. Andy screamed and lunged into the band of frightened horses.

Jim leaped off his horse, grabbed Curly's upraised arm, spun him around and felled him with a hard blow to the jaw. "Never touch that mule again!" Jim raged as he stood over the prostrate cowboy.

Curly shook his head and rose to one knee. Then he stood up, as Jim backed off a few feet to show that he did not intend to hit him while he was down.

Curly's face was livid as he raised his quirt and advanced on Jim threateningly.

Jim unsheathed his knife. "Drop that whip," he said, "and take off your gun belt."

"You're gonna get it, kid," Curly growled. "If you've got the guts to put that knife down, you're gonna get it good.'"

"Not with that whip, I'm not. Neither Andy or me's gonna take any more of that, now or any other time. Now drop it!"

Curly pulled the loop off his wrist and let his plaited leather quirt fall to the ground. Then, unbuckling his gun belt and dropping it to the ground, he stepped away from his weapons and glared at Jim. "Now what?" he demanded contemptuously.

Jim knew that he was no match for the burly cowboy and that his first punch had caught the man off guard when he was too angry to care, but Curly had shaken off the effects of that blow and now it was his turn.

Jim raised his fists and awaited the advancing man. His wiry strength was not equal to that of the heavy-muscled foreman, and he knew that he had to stay away from him. Standing flat-footed until Curly was two steps away, Jim made a move as though to back away, then as Curly lunged, he stepped aside and hooked his left fist against Curly's face with all the power he could throw into his punch. But he missed Curly's chin and hit his ear with a painful but not decisive blow.

Curly bellowed angrily as he floundered past Jim, half-stumbled, and tried to spin around to catch his young opponent.

Jim took advantage of the opportunity, forgetting his decision not to close in with the stronger man, and leaped upon Curly's back, driving him to the ground. The foreman's face ploughed into the hard ground, and Jim tried to pin him down.

That was a mistake, and Jim knew it the moment he felt the powerful surge of Curly's muscular shoulders. The cowboy broke Jim's hold, and before the boy could leap clear, he felt himself encircled by muscular arms. Overpowered, he knew that he had lost the fight.

Curly snarled, grabbed Jim's hair in both hands, and violently smashed his face into the hardpacked ground

95

again and again with brutal, merciless fury. Jim lost consciousness, and still the cowboy continued to pound his face into the dirt.

"That's enough, Curly!" Ace yelled as he tried to pull the foreman off his battered, helpless victim. "You don't have to kill the boy."

The *segundo* broke away and again slammed Jim's face against the ground, then turned his head around by the hair and examined the bleeding face. He spat on the ground and said, "That'll take the starch out of this big-mouthed hillbilly."

"That makes you proud?" Ace asked sarcastically.

"You takin' a hand in this, Ace? I whipped you once, and I'd be glad to oblige again," Curly threatened.

"You've whipped every man in this outfit, except the Old Man and Frisco," Ace admitted. "Now you've whipped a helpless old mule and a spunky kid who ain't old enough to shave. You ain't provin' much today, Curly."

The other hands nodded in agreement. Curly knew that they would not gang up on him, but he also knew that he was losing face with these men. He turned to Moose.

"Take care of the kid," he said. "He's your partner."

Moose glared at the foreman, knelt beside Jim, and shook his head angrily as he saw what Curly had done to his young friend.

Frisco came up with a pan of hot water, a clean cloth, and some disinfectant. Gently he washed the grime and clotted blood from the boy's face.

"I thought his nose was broke," Moose said, "but I reckon it's just swole."

The water revived Jim, and he tried to stand up.

"Easy, son," Frisco said. "We got some patchin' to do, before you'll be ready to get up and about."

Too sick to argue, Jim sank back and let Frisco work on his face. The cook was gentle, but he was also very thorough, and the process was painful. In spite of himself, Jim flinched.

"Sorry, son," Frisco said, "but it's got to be done. Texas air is pure, and there's no healthier place in the world than right here on this prairie. But I wouldn't want to vouch for this particular piece of ground where the cattle and horses have been messin' around. Lay still and let me finish the job."

Painstakingly, he scrubbed the last particles of dirt from the boy's lacerated face, thinking not only of the possibility of blood poisoning, but of the likelihood that if any grime were in the cuts, it would tattoo Jim's face when the flesh healed. Finally, he applied a powerful disinfectant.

"Eee-YOW!" Jim howled. "What is that stuff — horse liniment?"

"It's good for what ails you," was Frisco's noncommittal reply.

Jim could stand no more. He pushed Frisco aside, thanked him, and walked toward Andy. Still feeling groggy, he staggered slightly.

"Where do you think you're goin'?" Frisco asked. "You're too sick to work."

"Could be, maybe," Jim admitted, "but I'm sure too sick to lay there and take any more of your doctorin'. Two more minutes of that and I'd be dead — or wish I was."

"You took quite a beating, Jim. What made you think you could whip Curly?"

"I never thought I could, but I sure wasn't gonna let him hurt Andy. If he ever tries that again I'll take a club to him. I mean that, Frisco."

There was a welt across the mule's face that made Jim forget his own pain. "I'm sorry, Andy," he said as he gently touched the injured area.

Then Jim remounted Dancer and drove the band back to the night pasture. Traveling in ever-widening spirals, he accounted for the tracks of all of the horses he had rounded up earlier and sorted them out until he found a trail which he believed to have been made by the white-stockinged sorrel and his companion.

He studied the trail and read many signs. The sorrel was hobble-wise. He knew how to hold his shackled fore-legs together and hop along almost as well as though he had been completely free. The other animal had stayed with him. Jim decided that next time he would hobble the second horse instead of the sorrel.

Convinced that these were the tracks he wanted, Jim followed them at a gallop. In less than twenty minutes he had located the strays grazing contentedly on grass that was no better than that which they had left behind.

He shook out a loop and approached them. The hobbled horse saw him coming and concealed his ability, becoming a pitiful sight as he pretended to stumble and falter with each awkward lunge against the hobbles.

Jim broke into a grin that hurt his battered face.

"You're a fake," he said good-naturedly, as he dismounted. The horse stood quietly as Jim unhobbled him and then patted his neck. Cutter was a beautiful animal.

Jim drove the two horses back to the remuda and staked out Cutter's companion so he wouldn't stray. Then he fashioned a halter with the end of his lariat and led Cutter up the trail.

"Where you goin' with him?" Frisco called from the back of the chuck wagon as Jim started to ride past.

"Curly said he wants him right away. I'm taking him up to the point."

"Don't you know Curly rode him all yesterday afternoon? He'll want to give him a rest today."

"I know that, but I want to let him know I know it. He made a big fuss about wanting this horse, and he's gonna get him."

"Better let it lay, Jim," Frisco advised quietly. "You showed up better than you might think you did. No sense in pressin' your luck."

Jim smiled, hesitated, then released the animal with a friendly pat.

"How about some chow, Frisco? I ain't 'et yet."

"Well, you've been a busy boy, Jim. I reckon I can rustle up somethin' for you if you're sure you've worked up an appetite."

He threw a steak in the pan while Jim staked out

Dancer. He started to whistle, but his lips were too badly swollen. He hummed a cheery tune as he walked to the chuck wagon.

Jim had no idea why his friend smiled at him, but he responded with a lopsided grin. His face hurt, and his head throbbed like a beating tomtom, but he felt good.

## 9

The Chisholm Trail began in a fan-shaped network of tracks left by longhorns gathered from herds ranging along the Rio Frio, the San Antonio, Nueces and the Guadalupe Rivers. They were driven northward toward Fort Worth where, like streams joining a great river, the tributary paths converged to form the main trail to Abilene.

The famous cattle-way was a sinuous, many-veined system of hoof-beaten paths scouted by trail bosses responsive to the ever-changing conditions of weather and terrain.

Where either uniformly good or bad conditions prevailed over vast areas, offering the trail bosses little choice, there were many parallel trails marking the minor variations to the east or west according to individual preferences of the men who led each drive.

But where easy going, good crossings, or grass and water made one route clearly the best, all paths converged to make a deep-trodden trail which in some places became a wide, shallow trench.

Jim rarely saw Tom Peters during the day, but he soon learned the importance of the rancher's scouting ahead of the herd to select the best routes and bedding grounds. Even though they nibbled at the grass as they walked, the longhorns needed the good grass and rest they were given at the end of each day's march. A lot of savvy went into the handling of a cattle drive.

The steers were now accustomed to the routine of the trailing. By the time the sun rose each day, they were grazing northward; each in his relative position within the undulating column. There was no real line. The trail-broken animals fanned out or converged according to the terrain, and the flankers did not exercise unnecessary restraint upon them. All day, every day, the longhorns walked northward.

"Man, it's dusty!" Jim said to Frisco as he pulled up beside the chuck wagon for a palaver. "We sure could use a good rain right now. Does it ever rain out here?"

"Yeah, and when it does you'll be ridin' chin-deep in mud, and the dust'll still be blowin' in your face. That's Texas weather."

"The critters are gettin' pretty thirsty, Frisco. They're tongue-swole, red-eyed, and ringy."

"That they are, but the Red River's just a half-day ahead. You're in for your first deep-water crossin'."

Jim had heard many stories about how thirst-maddened longhorns stampeded when they caught the scent of distant water, but the drovers showed no concern.

About two miles south of the river, the drovers threw the herd off the trail in good pasturage where there was no danger of their mixing with any other herd that might come up to the crossing.

While the cowboys were gathering the longhorns, Jim hobbled some of his band and set the remuda out in good graze.

He made it a point always to be last in line at the chuck wagon tail gate, because he figured that the other men not only were his seniors, but they were more apt to be called back on the job for any of the many emergencies which came up to make a drover miss a meal or a night's sleep.

Cowboys had to "sleep fast" during a cattle drive. After fourteen hours in the saddle every day, they slept six hours — if they were lucky — then spent four hours night-herding. Nobody had to push these men. They knew what had to be done, and the deep loyalty of cowboys for their brand made them do what needed doing without question. But that did not stop them from constantly grousing about the lives they led.

"Who gave you the poor advice to become a cowpoke, instead of seekin' a more pleasant career, like raisin' skunks for profit and pleasure?" Ace Dawson asked Jim.

"How can you ask the boy a question like that, Ace?"

Moose chided his friend. "We all love our work. Me, I wouldn't trade places with any man on earth — unless I had the chance. Jim was real smart — joinin' up with this outfit. It's a wonderful life — for that Andy mule of his."

"I guess it was Andy's idea," Jim agreed. "I was unconscious when Frisco picked me up. Before I recovered from my delirious condition, he talked me into this degrading work. Andy took to wranglin' horses before I was even out of the bunk, and that gave Frisco the idea."

"It was a good idea, too," Frisco cut in. "Thanks to me, we've got the best horse-handler this outfit ever had."

"Why, thanks, Frisco," Jim said. "I really don't deserve that kind of praise."

"You sure don't! I was talkin' about Andy," Frisco said with a malicious grin, as the hands hooted with laughter.

"I won't argue that point," Jim said. "I'll play second fiddle to Andy any day in the week."

"A man's known by the friends he keeps." Curly's sarcastic tone chilled the group's good humor.

"Count your friends, Curly!" Frisco said harshly. "Do you want every man here who likes you to show it by raisin' his right hand, right now?"

A hush fell over the men. The blood drained from Curly's face. He walked over to the chuck wagon and put his empty plate on the tail gate, in violation of the unwritten law of the cattle trail that requires every man to scrape his plate and put it into the wreck pan to be washed. No man except the cook is permitted to use the tail gate.

Curly was dangerously angry. Jim wondered why he didn't challenge Frisco, or even fire him. As *segundo*, he must have the authority to dismiss a cook — even a good trail cook. The hands would have resented the loss of Frisco, but that didn't seem like enough reason to stop Curly in his present mood.

The fine edge had gone from what had promised to be a pleasant evening. The men drifted away to their various tasks, and Jim helped Frisco clean up the chuck wagon.

"Thanks for siding with me, Frisco, but you didn't have to do that," Jim said.

"Let it lay," Frisco said grimly.

After he had checked his remuda and assured himself that all the horses were present and contentedly grazing, Jim rode over to the bedding ground where Moose was night-herding. Jim sang as he approached, so Moose and the cattle would know he was coming.

"Howdy, Jim," Moose said. "Yo're in good voice tonight. I recognize the tune, but the words don't seem familiar."

"They're the words that were written for the song, Moose."

"Well, small wonder I didn't know 'em! I been singin' the names of our horses to that tune so long I forget they ain't the right words."

"You're joshing, Moose."

"No, I ain't. None of the boys know the words of the songs they sing. Mostly they just sing whatever they think of the world in general and cow-herdin' in par-

105

ticular. Some of the less inventive boys sing writin' they've memorized."

"Like the words of a poem?"

"More likely the words wrote on a can label or in a catalog. Listen to Dusty on the next passin'."

The pair of night herders rode in opposite directions as they circled the band, so they passed each other twice during each circuit. Jim listened attentively as he rode with Moose. The distant voice was faint at first and grew louder as they drew closer to the singer. Finally, Jim was able to make out the words, and he could hardly believe his ears.

Dusty was singing a classical melody. Jim had never heard its original words, but he was sure they were not those he was now hearing:

"Number three-hundred and ten; plain seat; steel horn; Cantle covered with roll; russet stock saddle; double rigged; two cinches; two-inch latigos; forty dollars without tapaderos; forty-five dollars with tapaderos . . ."

"Dusty is hurtin' for a new stock saddle, and from the way he sings, I'll lay odds he'll shell out the extra five dollars for the one with tapaderos," Moose said.

"Well, I'll be dogged," Jim said. "I'll be diddly-dad-dogged. You don't have to be a mind reader to get the goods on a night herder, do you?"

"Not if you can stomach his singin'," Moose agreed.

"How's it going, Dusty?" Jim greeted, as they passed the singing night herder.

"Beats gettin' jabbed in the eye with a sharp stick, Jim," Dusty responded cheerfully, "but not by more'n a little bit."

Moments later, they heard him again singing his song of love for a saddle.

"Moose, why'd Curly let Frisco rawhide him tonight? I figured he'd stomp him for that. He sure looked mad enough to do it, and he's sure mean enough to beat up a cripple."

"But he's not crazy enough, if that cripple happens to be Frisco," Moose said.

"You mean the men would do something about it if he tried?"

"The men would hold back until they was asked to take a hand — which they wouldn't be. Around these parts, we let a man fight his own battles, unless he needs help and asks a friend for it. Curly's afraid of Frisco."

"Why?" Jim asked with disbelief. "Curly's younger, stronger and tougher, and he's not crippled, like Frisco. What's he got to fear?"

"Frisco's the best gun around here. Except for a few professional killers, he's probably the best gun in Texas."

"I've never seen him wear one."

"If you do, it won't be for purposes of decoration. There's a lot to Frisco. He's been a heap of places and done a lot of things, but don't get the idea he's a drifter or a saddle tramp that knows nothin' better than mixin' up a batch of sourdough biscuits. Nobody much blamed Curly for walkin' away from that fracas — he showed practically suicidal courage leavin' his plate on the tail gate the way he did. If Frisco'd taken it into his head to call him on that, Curly'd have been up the crick."

"Did Frisco ever kill a man, Moose?"

"If he wants you to know about that, he'll tell you hisself," Moose said roughly, "but I wouldn't advise askin' him right out."

"Sorry, Moose," Jim said. "Forget I asked that one."

"It's forgotten, Jim, but here's somethin' for you to remember: watch out for Curly. Now he'll be dangerous as a froth-mouthed wolf. You keep makin' him look bad."

"I don't mean to," Jim said. "I'll try to pacify him. I don't need an enemy in this outfit."

"Better if you just stay outa his way. The last thing Curly craves is to make peace with you. Be careful. Be *real* careful!"

"Thanks for the warning, Moose. I'd better bed down my cavvy now," Jim said.

"My pleasure, Jim. We didn't do much today — "

" — but we'll sure give 'er hell tomorrow," Jim replied to the standard lead with the customary response.

Dancer was a joy to ride in the daytime and an absolute privilege at night. Alert, but never inclined to shy; smart, fast, surefooted, and gentle — unless abused, the spunky cow pony had earned Jim's affection and respect.

He circled the band to assure himself that all was well, then bedded down for a good sleep until the time came for his after-midnight round.

The following morning, after the cowboys had cut out their mounts, Tom Peters hunkered down beside Jim as he was eating breakfast.

"I want you to bring the remuda out ahead of the herd this morning, Jim. Frisco will join you with the chuck wagon, and you two will cross the river ahead of the herd. I'll meet you at the crossing and tell you what to do."

Jim was excited at the prospect of being where he could watch the deep-water crossing, instead of bringing up the rear after the job was done. The remuda was grazing in good order, so he had time to help Frisco prepare the chuck wagon. He lost no time in opening a barrage of questions.

"Do they always send the chuck wagon and remuda ahead on crossings, Frisco?"

"Not always. The Old Man likely wants you to help with the herd and figures to get the band over on the north bank out of the way. I can set up for the nooning and have chow ready by the time the boys swim the cattle across."

"Will it be a hard crossing?"

"Could be. It's my guess the river's bank-full and runnin' fast. Anything can happen when longhorns hit deep water. They can swim like seals. With good handlin' and a lot of luck, we can cross 'thout losin' a steer-brute. But if we mess the job, that river can fill up with enough dead steers for a man to walk from bank to bank on their backs 'thout wettin' his boots."

"What all can happen, Frisco?" Jim asked, as he finished swabbing out a big iron kettle.

"Anythin', Jim, and everythin'. This crossin' is popular; you've seen how many trails come a fannin' in this way from fifty or sixty places where Texas drives commence. So maybe another herd'll come up just when we get there. But with Tom Peters up front, we should be all right on that score. He probably can head off another outfit unless some greenhorn trail boss brings up a herd 'thout scoutin' ahead.

"The Old Man timed the drive so we'd get there when the sun will be too high to shine on the water and dazzle the steers. But the carcass of some drowned critter could float by just as the first steers hit the water. That could make 'em turn back and start the herd to millin' — we could lose a lot of cattle and some men in a stampede at the riverbank. Anythin' could happen, Jim. You dream up the wildest, weirdest, most outlandish, impossible thing you can think of, and you can be sure it's happened at a river crossin'."

Frisco drove his four-horse team faster than usual, and Andy kept the remuda right behind the chuck wagon. It wasn't long until the mile-long herd of steers disappeared in the distance behind them, and nothing could be seen of them but a dust cloud that hung over the trail and marked their progress.

Jim pulled up alongside the chuck wagon. "Frisco," he said, "this is the first time I knew you could trail-drive a herd of longhorns without eating a peck of Texas dust every mile. Feels good to breathe air again."

"Enjoy it while you can, Jimmy boy, tomorrow mornin' we'll be pullin' up the rear again. Many's the time I've heard men say that the Chisholm Trail moves every time a herd passes over it. It goes up in dust and by the time it settles back to earth, the trail might be a half-mile east or west of where it was the day before — dependin', of course, which way the wind is blowin'."

"I believe every word you say," Jim answered. "As a matter of fact, yesterday I was galloping back to hunt a stray, and before I knew what happened, Dancer ran right off the dust cloud we'd been ridin' on and fell eight feet to the ground. It's a miracle one of us didn't break a leg."

"Jim, you're a pure Texan," Frisco said admiringly. "You can tell Texas-facts along with the best of 'em now."

"That's because I have the benefit of good teaching, Frisco. You taught me all I know," Jim replied with a grin.

"Well, don't get it into your head that I'm braggin' about that, Jim. I don't picture you as a livin' monument to mark my passin' through this world."

"How about teaching me to shoot, when we have more time?"

"You can hit anythin' you point that Kentucky rifle of yours at, Jim. You need shootin' lessons like a mossyhorn needs teachin' how to stompede."

"I mean a pistol, Frisco. I've been told you're the best shot in these parts, and I want to learn how to handle a gun. The rifle's fine for the Tennessee hills, but it sure gets in the way when I try to rope a critter."

"You aimin' to gun somebody?"

"No, but I need a gun in my work, and you know it. How 'bout it, Frisco? After the drive, we'll have time, and I'll have the money to buy some ammunition."

"We'll see, Jim. Right off, we've got a cattle drive to

occupy our time, and until we push the last longhorn across the river, we'd better give our thoughts over to the crossin'."

"There's the river, now!" Jim cried, sighting a distant line of cottonwoods that marked the river's course.

"Here comes the Old Man," Frisco said, as the rancher rode toward them at a gallop.

Tom led them to the crossing site. The steers would have to swim most of the way across the brimful river, but he had chosen a sloping bank where they could wade in — rather than have to be driven off the edge of a bank and made to plunge into the fast-flowing stream.

"Let's get the chuck wagon across while the horses are watering," Tom Peters said. "There's a couple of logs on the bank."

Frisco drove the chuck wagon to the crossing site, where they unloaded about half of the supplies it carried. They lashed a log to each side of the vehicle to increase its buoyancy, then Tom Peters and Jim secured their lariats to the chuck wagon and preceded it into the roily river. Frisco yelled, cracked his whip above the backs of his two lead horses, and away they went!

The current was strong, but Dancer and Tom Peters' buckskin pony held their footing and waded out ahead of the team until they were swim-deep. Then the two horses struck out for the far shore. Trailing their long lariats behind them, Tom and Jim prepared to exert the strength of their mounts when the need arose.

Climbing the north bank just as the wagon team reached swimming depth, they worked their way to dry land and good footing. When the wagon's progress gave them enough slack on their lariats, they turned and watched it advance.

Frisco was yelling and cracking his whip, and the four horses swam well. The lead horses reached the shore and scrambled for secure footing on the slippery mud bank as the chuck wagon wheels touched down on the soft river bottom. Now the problem was to keep the vehicle moving to maintain momentum when the going became hardest. Jim dug his heels into Dancer's flanks and the cow pony responded with all the strength of his short-coupled, well-muscled body. Tom's buckskin mount did the same, and the two lariats strained against the weight of the heavy wagon. Without the aid of the two saddle horses, the chuck wagon team would never make it up the riverbank. Even with the added power, the outcome was uncertain.

Jim could feel Dancer's muscles writhe beneath the saddle, and the rope, taut as a bowstring, pressed hard against his leg. The chuck wagon slowed down, almost stopped. Frisco yelled louder and again cracked his long whip. The team lunged against their traces, and slowly the wagon wheels broke free from the mud and rumbled up the north bank and out on the plain.

"Good work!" Tom said. "The going got a little rough for a minute there."

He and Jim made a second trip across the river, fetching the supplies they had unloaded from the chuck wagon before crossing. It didn't take long for them to reload. Then Jim retrieved his rifle and strapped it across his shoulder with the thong he had attached to it for that purpose.

Tom Peters looked approvingly at the care the boy took of his weapon, even though he did not approve of the rifle as a handy side arm for one of his hands. The two of them towed the logs back to the south bank for the benefit of the next outfit to come up the trail.

Tom Peters gave Jim his instructions. "Find a good holding place off the main trail, about two miles north of here, and put the horses out to graze. Hobble some of them, like you do at night. Then come back. Frisco will stay with the chuck wagon, where you pasture the remuda, and get chow ready."

## 10

From afar, the herd looked like an army of marching ants, an irregular formation within which individuals meandered, but only far enough to swell the column out on one side or draw it in on the other.

Hoofs pounded, horns clattered, and steers bellowed impatiently as they smelled the water. This was a crucial moment. Twelve hundred half-wild, thirsty longhorns rumbled toward the river like a disaster looking for an excuse to happen. It would not take much to trigger them into a stampede.

Riding point, Curly and Ace warily flanked Big Red, prepared for anything, guiding him without pressure.

"Ride upriver a couple hundred yards, Jim," Tom

Peters said. "Keep your eyes peeled. Don't let anything come down to the crossing. It's important."

Patrolling the north bank, Jim scanned the swollen, muddy river for a half-mile above the crossing. There he stopped, carefully searched the river for floating objects all the way up to the distant bend. Satisfied, he turned back to watch the advancing longhorns.

Big Red warily approached the river. He sniffed, peered, edged forward, pawed the ground, and snorted gustily. Behind him surged the clamorous herd, impatient, irritable, and dangerously anxious. Jim found it hard to turn away from the critical situation at the riverbank, but he dutifully looked upstream and carefully scanned the surface all the way to the bend.

Finally, the lead steer entered the swirling water and waded out until he stood knee-deep in the swift current. There he stopped to drink. Other longhorns swarmed into the stream until thirsty cattle jammed the shallow, blocking the way of onrushing brutes behind them.

Curly and Ace, braving the fearsome array of tossing, gleaming horns, waded their surefooted mounts through the mass of close-packed cattle. The steers gave way under their insistent pressure, and the two cowboys eased the leaders out to swim-depth and pointed them toward the north bank.

This was a dangerous moment. Jim knew that if anything happened right now to make those lead steers double back on those entering the water, the river would become a whirlpool of frantically milling longhorns. Men and beasts would die there.

116

He swept the turbid river with anxious eyes, afraid that he might miss something which would scare the herd into a deadly mill. Relieved to see that the water surface was unbroken all the way up to the bend, he started to turn away. Then he saw something that chilled him.

A water-soaked log barely rippled the surface of the turbulent river as it drifted ponderously — a great, shadowy bulk, almost completely submerged in the muddy water. Huge, heavy, and menacing, its presence would surely panic the longhorns.

Jim knew that he could not make his voice heard above the bellowing of the cattle. Firing his rifle might warn the men — it might also stampede the herd. The log must be stopped before it reached the crossing, and only he could stop it!

Heeling Dancer into a dead run, Jim shook out a wide loop and swung it overhead, as he raced to intercept the waterborne menace. Pulling up at the water's edge, Jim saw that the huge log was smooth. There was no projecting limb or root over which he could cast his loop.

He had to go into the river and tie his rope around the log. Jim thought that he could swim out to it but doubted that he would be able to see the submerged log, once he entered the water.

He dismounted, put aside his rifle, and pulled off his shoes. Quickly, he leaped into the saddle. Without hesitation, Dancer plunged into the raging Red River.

Jim snubbed the end of the rope to his saddle horn and shook out a small loop.

The cow pony swam close to the log, but Jim could

not reach it from the saddle. He came closer; the log butted Dancer's shoulder with a bruising jar that drove the brave animal downstream.

Jim heeled the pony's flank. With courageous devotion to duty, which surpassed his pain and fear, Dancer again came in close. An eddy swung the log and again it crashed against his thrashing legs.

Jim could not urge the animal to endure any more abuse. Taking the rope end off the saddle horn, he headed Dancer shoreward and slipped out of the saddle into the water. A few powerful strokes took him to the log. He wrapped an arm half around its slimy bulk while easing the rope around one end. Then, making certain that he had not fouled his lariat, he kicked off and swam shoreward, playing out the rope's coils as he fought against the powerful current.

But he was not swimming fast enough. The force of the river bore him downstream toward the frightful jam of flashing horns and flailing hoofs. He tied the rope end around his waist to free both arms for swimming.

Tiring rapidly, he gasped for breath and gulped a throatful of water, choked, raised his hands overhead frantically and sank below the surface of the muddy water. But as the river closed over his head, he kicked downward, desperately fighting for air, and his feet hit the riverbed. He was at wading depth!

He staggered shoreward and saw that he could not reach Dancer without releasing his hold on the rope — which he dared not do. He called, then whistled, but the horse just flicked his ears.

Jim dug his stockinged heels into the ground and tried to pull the water-sodden log ashore, but he could not even hold it against the power of the river.

Then he saw a cottonwood tree which overhung the river edge. It was very close to the herd, but now Jim was so desperate that any chance for success was worth taking. He played out all the rope he could get and walked toward the tree as fast as he could — which was the speed at which the current bore the log downstream.

Jim heaved with all his might, trying to get a little more slack, but the relentless power of the river was too much for his waning strength. Ignoring the pain of his rope-burned hands, Jim heaved and yanked until he had gained enough slack rope to dally the lariat around the tree and snub it securely.

He reached beyond the tree with his left hand and pulled with it while he held the dally in his right. Heaving and snubbing until his muscles ached and his hands were raw, he worked on the rope, encouraged by the realization that he was gaining a little; not much, but even a few inches could be decisive. Now the log was directly downstream from the cottonwood, but a bend in the river prevented it from beaching, so Jim worked on, pulling and snubbing to gain every inch he could.

He had stopped the log far enough above the herd so that none of the longhorns would be spooked by it. However, as more animals crowded into the river, they fanned out, and it would not be long before they spread enough to reach the log's present position. Jim had to beach that log!

He waded into the stream, where he could get more leverage, and pulled the rope as hard as he could. But he gained only a couple of inches, and he knew that he was too tired to make any real progress. He secured the loose end of the rope and ran over to Dancer. Then he rode down to the crossing and found Tom Peters.

The rancher took in Jim's appearance with a swift glance, knew that this was an emergency, and did not waste time asking questions. He spurred his horse and followed Jim back to the log, where he sized up the situation and reached for his lariat.

Jim plunged into the river. Tom Peters tossed the lariat loop to him; Jim secured it to the lower end of the log. Then he stood clear, while the rancher dallied the free end of the lariat around his saddle horn and pressed his horse into action. The roping horse dug in and tugged until the log reached the bank, and there Jim put his shoulder behind it. Gradually, they worked it out of the river.

Jim unfastened the two lariats and remounted Dancer.

"Where you going?" Tom Peters yelled.

"Back up the river," Jim replied over his shoulder, as he galloped away. "There may be another log coming down."

The rancher nodded his silent approval. Then he returned to his job at the river crossing.

The last steers straggled across the Red River before Jim left his post to help the dragman clear the river of reluctant steers.

When the weary, bruised young wrangler finally arrived at the chuck wagon, most of the hands had finished eating. Tom Peters put his own plate down and held one out for Frisco to fill as soon as he saw the boy coming. Jim was surprised and more than a little embarrassed when the rancher handed him the food.

"Thanks, Mr. Peters," he said. "Thanks, kindly."

He grinned at Frisco and exchanged "howdys" with him.

"You did a good job back there, Jim," Tom Peters said. "We'd have been in real trouble, if you hadn't caught that log when you did."

The Old Man looked closely at Jim, then stood up and walked over to him. "You look like you'd been run over by a stampede, Jim. Let me see your hands."

Jim put his plate down and revealed his raw, rope-burned palms.

The rancher whistled softly.

"They look a lot worse than they feel, Mr. Peters."

"They'll feel a lot worse than they look by tomorrow, unless we do something about it," the rancher responded. "Frisco, have you got anything in your chest that might do the trick?"

"Sure have, and I've an extra pair of gloves that'll fit Jim. Should've thought of that before."

Tom Peters stepped into one of Jim's tracks in the dust. His boot covered Jim's footprint except for the wide heels and round toes of the boy's shoes. "And I've an extra pair of boots for you."

"I can get along with what I have," Jim said with more pride than understanding. "I'll buy what I need in the first town we hit after payday. Thanks, anyway."

"Now don't get your dander up. Frisco and I'd like to think we're your friends. We have something you need and we can spare. You can't handle a rope without gloves on your beat-up hands, and those shoes of yours are going to get you dragged someday. A cowboy needs the right gear to do a good job."

Meanwhile, Frisco had brought out the well-worn, soft, buckskin gloves and handed them to Jim. He pulled them on and, even though his hands were sore and swollen, the gloves were comfortable.

"Thanks, Frisco, these feel fine. I don't think I'll need any medicine on my hands now that I have these."

"Take 'em off, Jim. You're gonna get a dose of Doc Frisco's special ointment right now. It's good for what ails you."

He put a gob of thick, greasy salve in the palm of each of Jim's hands. Jim suspected that it was made of bear grease and something else, but he did not ask.

"Rub that stuff in good. It'll heal your burns, reduce the swelling, put hair on your chest, and help you see in the dark."

"I don't know if I'll see any better, but I'll smell a lot worse. Folks'll know I'm coming long before I'm within sight or hearing. WHEW!"

"Any medicine worth anythin's got to smell bad and taste bad," Frisco said. "Otherwise it's no account at all."

"Then this stuff must be plumb miraculous in its curing power. It's got the authority to make a skunk go into hiding. And don't even talk about tasting it — ugh!"

122

"Is that boy giving you trouble, Frisco?" Tom Peters asked as he returned. "Here, Jim, try these on for size."

He started to hand Jim the boots, then noticed his greasy hands and sniffed noisily. "You think that stuff's all right, Frisco? It smells like something crawled into it and died."

"Keep on a-talkin' like that, Tom, and you'll wind up cookin' for this outfit. Nobody says anything against my chow or my doctorin'," Frisco growled.

Tom Peters winked at Jim. "See if you can do anything to improve Frisco's disposition. Any change will help. I'll leave it to you. I've got to go back to work."

Jim examined the boots. The Old Man had talked as though they were a pair of spares he kept for any emergency, but they were brand new and of better quality than those which the rancher was wearing. He had given Jim his best pair.

"I can't take these," Jim told Frisco. "They're too good."

"The Old Man wants you to have 'em. Let's see how they fit."

Jim pulled off his shoes and was about to put on his new boots when Frisco stopped him. "Let me give you a hand," he said. "Your hands are slippery."

"Besides which, they'd smell high for a month if I got any of your skunk grease on them," Jim added with a grin.

"That's about all the smart talk I want to hear out of you today. Sit down, and I'll pull 'em on for you."

When Jim first attempted to walk in his new boots,

he thought that he would fall on his face. The high heels angled him forward, off balance, and the narrow toes did not provide a good foundation on which to stand or walk.

"Now I know why cowboys never walk," he said. "They can't do it in these boots. No wonder they hang horse thieves out here."

"But they sure do the trick when you're ridin'. You'll find that out after you try 'em. After that, you'll never wear another kind of shoes."

He would never have a more beautiful pair. They were well made and decorated with designs stitched into the soft uppers, making them attractive as well as functional. They were boots which Jim could wear with pride. He strutted awkwardly around the chuck wagon; his bruises and burns forgotten.

"Tom Peters liked the way you handled your job out there," Frisco said. "He was talkin' about you when you rode up."

"I didn't do much of a job. That log mighty near got away from me more than once. I was plenty lucky."

"Right! But there's one real important quality a man likes to see in another man out here, Jim, and that's the determination to hold down the job he's supposed to do — no matter what odds build up against him. Tom put it right when he said you 'stayed with the herd.'"

## 11

This night, like every night of the past week, was oppressively hot. The air was motionless, stifling. Hopefully, Jim looked at the cloudy sky; a summer shower would bring welcome relief to men and animals.

Moose sang with little spirit as he approached. In the gloom of this dark night, Jim could make out little but the silhouette that man and horse made against the skyline as they reached the top of the little hill.

"Welcome to the party, Moose. What brings you out here?"

"There's a storm brewin', and you just might need a helpin' hand."

"I'm sure glad for your company, anyhow. I've sort

of been hopin' for rain, though. We need it bad."

"It won't be just rain. This is lightnin' weather, and I figure it'll be a humdinger. A man could just about reach up and punch a hole through them clouds. It's as dark as the inside of a black bull's belly out here, and it's gittin' blacker by the minute!"

Jim could not see the remuda, but he heard the reassuring ringing of Andy's bell, and he knew that none of the horses was far away. He could not remember a darker night, even in the deep woods back in Tennessee. He hoped that Dancer could see better than he could.

Suddenly, as though four thousand lanterns had been lighted simultaneously, the horns of every steer within sight bore shimmering balls of blue phosphorescence, a ghostly glow.

"My gosh! What's that, Moose?" Jim cried.

"It's fox fire. Take it easy."

Lightning flashed in the distance. A thunder clap brought the steers to their feet. Never had Jim seen a more eerie sight.

Although they looked weird in the ghostly glow, the horses did not seem unusually nervous. Moose began to ride slowly around the remuda, so Jim started to circle the horses in the opposite direction.

What effect was the fox fire having on the unpredictable steers? Surely they saw it dancing on each other's horns. Jim was surprised that some of the spookier steers had not already bolted.

Again the distant sheet lightning brought the herd into view and again the rumbling thunder followed the flash — only this time it sounded much closer to them.

Jim drew abreast of Moose as they met on their circuit of the band. "Will the Old Man put more drovers on the herd tonight?"

"I doubt it. I figure him and Curly will relieve the night herders and handle it by theirselves. This is purely stompede weather, and two top men can do more good in a stompede than a bunch of drovers can. This ain't a time for mistakes. All hell can break loose on a night like this, Jim."

The air was stifling and getting hotter. Mopping his brow, Jim wished for a cooling breeze.

A shattering bolt of forked lightning split the sky and crashed down into the bedding ground. An explosive roar of thunder broke the silence.

The longhorns reacted instantly. Horns clattered and hoofs rumbled as the herd stampeded.

"STOMPEDE!" Moose roared.

The ground shook, another clap of thunder broke as lightning again opened the sky. Then the rain came down in torrents. Lightning was reflected from the gleaming horns and wet hides of hard running cattle. Balls of fox fire seemed to leap from horn to horn as the cattle stampeded across the prairie. How they ran! Jim was awed by the momentum of the massed steers. It seemed to him that nothing could turn or stop this terrible stampede of wild longhorns. Between flashes of lightning, he could see only the fire balls on their horns.

The storm raged with awesome intensity. Brilliant lightning flashes illuminated the scene briefly, then it was plunged into darkness that showed only the dull illumination of the fox fire.

"What shall we do, Moose?" Jim yelled over the crash of thunder.

"Just do yore job. We'll take care of the remuda and let the Old Man worry about the herd. This ain't a time to mess up the detail."

Jim had only vague impressions of what was going on now. The alternating brilliance of lightning and darkness between flashes made clear vision impossible, and he was not sure of what he did see.

The herd was running away from the rise where Jim had bedded his horses. They appeared in a new position with each flash of lightning, then disappeared with every brief moment of darkness. In the alternating brilliance-darkness cycle, the herd seemed to advance jerkily.

"Looks like they're turning," Jim cried.

"Good! Once the boys get 'em runnin' in a circle, they'll wear 'emselves out. Watch out, though, they just might head right back here. Be ready to move yore hosses out in a big hurry."

Jim was so excited that he did not feel the discomfort of the soaking rain, nor did he become frightened by the lightning bolts which crashed into the ground so near to him. But Moose was more familiar with the danger of lightning on the plain.

"Let's get off this rise and stay off'n it," he bellowed. "This here's the highest place around and that's where lightnin' strikes. Move off, right now!"

No sooner had he spoken, than Jim saw a jagged bolt

of lightning crash into the summit of the hillock, not fifty yards away from where he rode Dancer. That was where he had intended to go next, to better see the herd. Jim could almost smell the heat of the flash.

He rode out to help move the band down to level ground. Another glance toward the herd showed that they were indeed being swung around into a great circle. Again, he could hear the rumbling hoofs over the crashing thunder. The herd was no longer running away from the hillock. Now they were swinging around, and soon they would be coming nearer.

Jim hurried his remuda toward the area to which Moose was leading Andy. Even now, the horses were following the big white mule, but Jim urged the stragglers to walk faster toward the far side of the hillock, where they would be out of sight of the stampeding herd. So far, the horses had not been affected noticeably by the stampede, but the storm was making most of them nervous.

Moose rode back to where Jim was bringing up the band; Andy was leading them to the far side of the hillock base. "You better go back where you can see the herd, Jim. So's you can come here for any hosses they might want in a hurry. Otherwise, them as need mounts won't know where to get 'em."

"Okay, Moose."

"Stay off the top of the hill. Don't be the highest thing around, or you won't last long."

"I'll keep that in mind. Thanks."

Jim went halfway to the top of the low hillock, then

rode around it until he again could see the herd. He was surprised at the distance they had covered while he was moving the band. Now they had swung around and were heading almost directly toward the hill. And they were coming fast!

He could see two drovers— he took them to be Tom Peters and Curly — riding hard alongside the leaders of the stampeding longhorns, trying to swing them into a complete circle. But it was a very wide circle, and it looked as though they would swing around the hillock and run right into the place where Moose was holding the band. They were running hard, each lightning flash brought them into sight much closer than the previous one. They appeared to be all horns as they ran toward Jim, and they were even more fearsome than the bolts of lightning which crashed into the hillock. Jim urged Dancer up to the crest where he would have the advantage of height to see better the action of the hard-running longhorns, and of his remuda which was just around the base of the hill.

The next lightning flash showed Jim what he feared most. The band was still at the base of the hill, and the herd was swinging around it. The rushing cattle were heading toward Moose and the remuda on a semicircular route that would mass them right into the band in less than a minute. The wind was blowing from the band toward the herd, and with the hillock between them, Jim was sure that Moose could not hear the rumbling hoofs above the crashing thunderclaps. The little drover had no idea that he was in the path of the longhorns and would not realize it until they were upon him.

Jim dug his heels into Dancer's flanks and rode the cow pony over the shoulder of the hill toward the band, trusting to the pony to keep them out of trouble on the rough ground that lay between them and the remuda.

The stampeding herd thundered ever closer, as they swung around the hill. Jim cut straight across their path. He had to arrive at Moose's holding place ahead of the herd! The rain drove into his face, cutting down what little vision he had, even when lightning illuminated the landscape. He had to depend entirely upon Dancer's night vision and surefootedness, but he knew that Dancer could not see well enough to make their rough ride anything but a very risky gamble.

Jim ignored the danger. All he knew was that his friend and the remuda were in grave peril — so were the cattle and the men who were trying to bring them under control. Only he was aware of the impending collision between men, cattle, and horses. It was up to him — to him and Dancer.

Again he slammed his heels into Dancer's flanks, and the horse responded with a burst of speed. They raced over the shoulder of the hill and down on the plain where the band was loosely held. In a lightning flash, Jim saw Moose a couple of hundred yards away. He reined Dancer toward the little cowboy.

Fortunately, Moose glanced in his direction, saw Jim and realized that something was wrong. Excitedly, Jim waved his arms and pointed back over his shoulder.

"They're coming this way!" he yelled, knowing that

his voice could not be heard above the sound of the storm.

At that moment, the longhorn leaders swung around the base of the hill. Moose spurred his mount into action and began rounding up the band.

Jim saw Andy's white hide shining against the background of wet earth and rode down to him. He tied Dancer's reins to the saddle horn to ensure that the horse would be free to run, then he leaped upon Andy's back.

He glanced back to seek instructions from Moose, who was working furiously on the other side of the band. The man did not look his way, so Jim had to act on his own initiative.

It seemed risky to try to outrun the herd at night. The hillock looked like an island in a stormy sea. Even though lightning played around its summit, he preferred it to the path of the stampeding longhorns. He rode Andy uphill, depending upon his mule's strong attraction for the horses to lead the remuda up the hill after him.

He looked back and saw that several of the horses were following him up the hill. They came fast as though sensing the urgency of the situation. But in the storm he could no longer see Moose, nor could he be sure how many of the horses were following him. Now there was nothing he could do but lead the band up the hill. Mounted bareback, and without a bridle, there was little he could do, even if he had a change of plan.

The herd thundered around the base of the hill and engulfed the place where the band had been gathered. Moose was nowhere in sight!

Indeed, this hillock was like an island rising out of a storm-tossed sea. The herd passed under Jim's high point. Two horsemen rode beside the point of the herd and tried to contain the leaders. Jim had the feeling that he might be kept up on the hill for a long time if Tom Peters and Curly should try to use it as a pivot around which to run the wild steers.

Jim had no trouble keeping the horses on the hill above the stampeding steers. He rode Andy just below the crest and maintained a circle of small circumference to hold the horses below the hilltop where the danger from lightning bolts was greatest, watching for any horses which might try to go over to the other side of the hill and down onto the plain, where they would be in the path of the longhorns. Although the ring around the hill had not yet been closed, it looked as though it would soon be completely encircled by the cattle.

Jim felt miserable, and he was afraid. It was a lonely place, and a target for the worst lightning bolts he had ever seen. As he looked down upon the horses immediately below him and upon the tossing, gleaming horns of the herd that passed farther below, he knew that he was trapped upon the hill and must remain there until the stampede ended, unless the crazed steers should decide to go over the top of the hill, which would be only a slight obstacle. If that happened, he and the horses would be engulfed in a sea of hoofs and horns.

The herd had now closed its ring around the hill and showed signs of weariness. During lightning flashes, Jim could see that they ran more slowly, and they tossed their terrible horns less wildly. He had the feeling that the stampede would not last much longer. The ground was soggy. The repeated passage of thousands of hoofs over the ground had made a quagmire around the base of the hill. It must also be tiring the horses of the two cowboys, but there was no indication that either of them would try to change horses. The inside rider probably could do so, if he wanted to stop long enough.

Finally, some of the rearmost steers stopped running and trotted disinterestedly. These were the slowest animals, those which ordinarily made up the drag on the cattle drive. The stronger brutes still ran doggedly, but with diminishing strength. The stampede was running down.

Jim was exhausted. Time passed very slowly, as he waited for the dawn. He was tired, soaking wet, and hungry; but most of all, he was worried about Moose. He had not seen him since the stampeding longhorns had separated them.

Sunlight revealed a scene of desolation unlike anything Jim had ever seen before. As far as the eye could see, the rich prairie grass had been ground into the mud. No blade, leaf, or twig remained upon the scene. Dead and injured steers lay in the deep mud. It was like a nightmare. The screaming of a horse was ended by the sharp report of a heavy pistol. Jim left his remuda on the hilltop and rode over to the chuck wagon, which automatically became the new camp.

"Howdy, Jim," Frisco greeted him as he rode up on Andy.

"Howdy, Frisco. Did you make out all right?"

"Fine, son."

"Have you seen Moose this morning?"

"No. I thought he was with you."

"We got separated by the herd when they swung around the hill. That was hours ago, and I ain't seen him since."

"Have a bait and a cup of coffee, Jim," Ace said, as he came from around the back of the chuck wagon. "We'll find him."

"If it's all the same to you, I'd rather not wait to eat."

"You'll eat first. We might be out for quite a spell."

"That's right," Frisco agreed emphatically. "It's ready to eat." He handed Jim a plate of hot food and a cup of coffee.

"Thanks, Frisco, this smells real good."

Nervously, Jim wolfed his breakfast, then dropped his utensils into the wreck pan. "I'd better saddle me a fresh horse, Ace. I'll be back in a couple of minutes."

"You can stop frettin', Jim; look behind you."

Moose was riding double with Shorty. The little drover dismounted, while Jim was running up to see whether he had been hurt. Moose was mud covered from head to toes, but he appeared to have lost none of his spirit as he hobbled toward the chuck wagon.

"Are you okay, Moose? Let me give you a hand," Jim said.

"I'm fine as frog's hair," Moose roared. "The only thing I need is a cup of hot coffee."

"What happened to you? I sure was worried."

135

"My hoss fell and throwed me. About half the herd ran right over me. I shore thought I was a goner, but I ain't even scratched. Had to shoot the hoss, though. Leg was broke."

"You mean those longhorns jumped over you?" Jim asked.

"Hundreds of 'em, over me and around me, all throwin' their legs every which way to keep from steppin' on me. I've heard of it happenin' that way, but I'd never of believed it." Moose shook his head. "They like to of scared me to death. I kin still hear them poundin' hoofs comin' down all 'round me. Man, that shore was a night!"

# 12

Suddenly they were there. No movement had been visible against the open skyline. There were no trees or bushes to conceal their approach, but there they were — four Comanche braves mounted on painted ponies just out of pistol range, watching the passage of the remuda.

"How'd they get here, Frisco?" Jim asked excitedly.

"I don't know. Probably snaked up some little draw we can't see from here."

"Will they give us any trouble?"

"Maybe they'll try to collect a coupla beeves later on, but I've seen buffalo signs — and when they can get buffalo, they don't crave beef. They're probably more interested in your remuda than they are in the herd, so you'd better be ready for most anythin' from now on."

Tom Peters joined them at the chuck wagon. "We've got company, boys," he said.

"What do they want, Tom?" Frisco asked.

"I was about to put the same question to you. I figure they just want to let us know we're being watched. I'm going over to try for a palaver with them, if they'll stand still."

"I'd like to go along with you, Mr. Peters."

"Can you stay behind me and do absolutely nothing but watch and listen no matter what happens — unless I tell you different?"

"Yes."

"Let's go."

Jim rode behind Tom Peters as they approached the Indians. His rifle was slung across his back. He did not touch it for fear of aggravating the Comanches. Having practiced swinging it around into firing position, he knew that he could do it rapidly if he had to do so.

Tom Peters raised his right hand. Jim followed his example, holding his rein hand high so the Indians could see that it, too, held no weapon.

The braves were armed with lances, bows and arrows, and shields. One of them also carried a rifle.

"I'll watch the one with the rifle," Jim said as they rode forward.

"Forget the rifle. Those bucks can get off a dozen well-aimed arrows in the time it would take him to reload. Chances are he's let it rust and foul-up so bad it'd be undependable anyhow."

The Comanches were powerfully built men, shorter than any Indians he had seen before. Jim doubted that any of them was more than five feet six inches tall.

When the rancher and his wrangler were within a hundred feet of the Indians, one of them signaled his companions and, with a fearsome yell, they spun their horses and raced across the prairie.

"Ki-yi-yi-yieee," they wailed as they dashed away, then wheeled and raced northward. Suddenly, all four of them slipped from the backs of their saddleless mounts.

Jim and Tom could see nothing of the Indians except their painted faces showing below the necks of their ponies as they rode by at full speed.

"Look at 'em ride!" Jim cried.

"There's none to beat those fellows on horseback," Tom Peters said. "Before our people got repeating pistols, the Comanches could whip us every time in an even fight. Their braves can shoot a man full of arrows before he can reload a musket. A good bowman can keep an arrow in the air all the time — before the first one hits the mark, the second one is on its way. They can ride those ponies at a full gallop and shoot like they were standing on the ground.

"They can even shoot from under their ponies' necks, riding the way they are right now. If one warrior gets a horse shot out from under him, another one will snap him up without even slowing down. They don't let their wounded braves get captured."

"They sure use short bows," Jim said. "They must be less than three feet long."

"That s the best size for horse-Indians, but they can drive an arrow clear through a buffalo. Never make the mistake of thinking a Comanche is at a disadvantage just because he's not packing a gun."

The Comanches wheeled and swung back toward Tom and Jim, howling and brandishing their weapons ferociously. Jim's hands moved toward his shoulder-slung rifle.

"Steady, boy," Tom cautioned. "Just sit there and let 'em come."

It was not easy, but Jim sat still in his saddle, holding Dancer close-reined, quietly talking to him while the savages charged.

They dashed to within a hundred feet of the white men, wheeled again, raced across the prairie, and vanished in the distance.

"Whew!" Jim said. "I don't know what they had in mind, but if they wanted to scare me, they did."

"They were just putting on a show — for us and for each other," Tom Peters said.

"Will they try for the horses?" Jim asked, trying not to show the concern he felt.

"I doubt it, but I'd plan on it if I were you. Comanches love good horses, and you can bet that those fellows sized up every animal in your remuda before they left. They probably picked out the ones they'll take if they get the chance."

Tom Peters rode off up the trail. Jim rejoined Frisco at the chuck wagon.

"What do you think of the Comanches?" Frisco

asked, as Jim reined Dancer to a walk beside the chuck wagon.

"They sure had me guessing. If I'd been out there alone, I probably would have taken a shot at them. Then I'd have been in a fix for sure."

"I doubt that you would, Jim; you're a pretty level-headed youngster. But if you had shot one of 'em, you'd look like a porcupine right about now."

"I reckon I'm going to have to get me a repeating pistol. My rifle shoots real straight, but it won't handle more'n one target at a time. I always figured that back in the woods I could hit and kill anything I aimed at, and if there was two, I could throw my knife at the second one and have a good chance of hitting the mark. Then, with a tree to hide behind or a thicket to dive into, I could make out until I had time to reload. But that won't work out here on the prairie. There's no place to hide."

"You're right. There's nothing a Comanche likes better than havin' his enemy ride away, tryin' to reload a gun. They can get a man that tries that every time."

"There's lots of things I have to get when we hit Abilene and I get paid. I guess a Colt and some bullets goes high on the list."

"You've never handled a gun, have you, Jim?"

"No, I've never handled one, except to heft it. I've never fired a shot from a Colt."

"I'll start learnin' you first chance I get. I can't make a gunslinger out of you, but I can get you to where you can hit a reasonable target at a reasonable distance within a reasonable time."

Jim grinned. "That sounds reasonable. Thanks."

Jim saw no more Comanches that day, but he kept alert and frequently left the trail to scout the vicinity for signs of Indians.

"I reckon those Comanches we saw are the only ones around these parts, Frisco," he said at supper that night.

"Chances are you're right, but don't be too sure. You didn't see 'em come up on us back there — none of us did. They could be all around us without showin' up unless they wanted to be seen."

"That's right, Jim," Moose joined in the conversation. "Them red rascals can be all around without you knowin' it. Remember, they can see our dust from miles away and keep track of us all the time — knowin' we can't leave the herd to scout Indians. So, if they want to give us trouble, they can pick the time and the place. We've got to be ready for 'em every minute — but we can't be."

Jim looked the ground over — a custom quickly learned in a land of rattlers, tarantulas, and scorpions — squatted, and balanced his tin plate on one knee. Moose sat at his left and Shorty at his right side. The tall Texan thumbed his sombrero to the back of his head and forked a load of beans into his wide mouth. Then he cut a big piece of steak and wadded it in with the beans. His cheeks bulged until his eyes looked like black slits peering out of his distended face. He took three fast chews, then gulped down a great mouthful. Another load of beans was popped into his mouth and another big chunk of steak.

Jim was an enthusiastic eater, but he offered no competition for this Texas giant. He watched Shorty, enthralled by the man's oral capacity and by the action of his prominent Adam's apple. Jim could feel his own throat constrict as, involuntarily, he helped the cowboy swallow each mouthful. Then, realizing that he still had not eaten a bite of his own food, he went to work on his plate — doing a pretty fair job of eating on his own.

The cowboys sitting around the fire were in a festive mood that night. Moose got out his guitar and, before long, all voices were raised in song. Little Moose sang a bullfrog bass and Jim was a middling fair baritone.

Ace took the lead, because he knew the melodies of all the songs that the men liked best and was able to start out any tune they mentioned. Shorty hit the high notes with the gusto of a man who fancies himself to be an undiscovered operatic tenor. Perhaps this was not the worst singing ever heard on a cattle drive, but a coyote sextet just might have sounded more melodious.

A long time had passed since last the cowboys had enjoyed any relaxation, so they took their fun where they found it, making the most of any chance to let off steam. Singing, joking, telling tall tales, proving their prowess with rope, gun, or in a wrestling match were their ways of having fun on the trail. Jim enjoyed every minute of it. Even the bad singing was pleasant when shared with men he liked.

"Shorty, you bray worse than old Andy," Ace commented as a song ended in howling failure, because Shorty's enthusiasm had exceeded his vocal range.

"I take that as an insult, Ace," the tall, tone-deaf Texan answered. "I've the voice of a lark, and I've a mind to make you admit that well-known fact."

"You've the voice of an asthmatic jackass," Ace said, "and you're not man enough to make me say anything different."

"Maybe you'd like talking thataway while I'm rubbin' your nose in the dirt," Shorty threatened.

Jim grinned as he joined the others in forming a ring within the firelight while the two belligerents circled each other like gladiators joined in mortal combat.

These men were two of the best wrestlers in camp. Ace was a powerful fellow; strength was apparent in every move of his massive arms and back, as muscles rippled under his tight shirt. He looked as though he could snap the spine of his beanpole opponent with a mighty bear hug.

But Shorty was deceptively strong. His stringy-looking muscles were like rawhide, and his long legs could squeeze the breath out of an opponent, once he wrapped them around him. And he was cat-quick.

"Throw him, Ace," Moose encouraged his choice of the moment. "Crack him like a whip!"

"Wrap yore laigs around that Ace, and cut him into a pair of deuces," another voice called from the ring of drovers.

The two cowboys continued to circle each other warily, each seeking a weakness in his opponent's defense, trying to draw him off guard.

Then Ace made his play, lunging at Shorty with his

head lowered and his arms outstretched. His lanky friend leaped aside just in time, grasped Ace's left wrist and swung himself upon the heavier man's broad back.

"Ride 'im, cowboy!" Frisco yelled.

"Buck 'im off, Ace," Moose encouraged, as Ace leaped, spun, and sunfished like a mustang, trying to dislodge his long-legged rider.

But the tall Texan's powerful legs were clamped around Ace's midsection like the coils of a boa constrictor. Within seconds, Ace was gasping for air.

"You win, cowboy," he wheezed. "Unwrap your legs; let me breathe."

"Who's the world's finest tenor?" Shorty demanded.

"You are. Turn me loose!" Ace gasped.

"That's right," Shorty agreed. "Now trot twice around the chuck wagon, and we'll call it quits."

Amidst the cheers and hoots of the men of the Tepee brand, Ace trotted twice around the wagon as Shorty slapped his hips with his Stetson and sang "Dixie" at the top of his voice — a voice which added anguish to the discomfort of his victim.

Jim left the campfire when the get-together broke up. Returning to the pasturage where he had left his remuda for the night, he saddled Nighthawk, Frisco's second-best night pony, and rode out to patrol the area.

First, he checked every horse to make sure that all of the saddle animals were at ease and that the remuda was complete. All of them appeared to be contented and unconcerned, which was a pretty good indication that no marauders were nearby.

But that was not enough to satisfy Jim — not after he had seen bold young Comanches in the region and learned that the horse-craving Indians had seen his remuda. These fine animals would offer a temptation which Comanches would not be apt to resist — a double temptation: to increase their wealth, and to experience the sheer joy of proving that they could spirit them away from white men.

Jim knew that it would be almost impossible to locate prowling Indians by searching the entire area afoot, as he had done on other nights. They would be hard to find in so vast a territory. He rode quietly, depending upon his horse to react to the sight, smell, or sound of strangers — or of unfamiliar horses.

The moon rose, the prairie brightened, and Jim could see almost as well as though it were twilight time. A rippling breeze increased the illusion that he was surrounded by a sea of grass. Jim saw the horses clearly. In the distance, he made out the cattle, which were bedded down on the slope of a slight rise in the prairie.

Jim examined the ground which he had selected for his bedsite before spreading his tarpaulin and blanket. Then he tied one end of the lariat around Nighthawk's neck and the other to his wrist. It seemed that all was well. He was ready to retire to his blanket, but he doubted that he could sleep very well in the bright moonlight.

He was wrong about that. Wearied by a long, hard day, he fell asleep the moment his head touched the blanket. Jim had foregone the comfort of using his saddle for a pillow, wanting to leave his horse saddled for instant readiness in case of an emergency. He would change mounts sometime after midnight, so Nighthawk would be given a rest without the weight of the saddle or the restriction of its cinch.

He slept a dreamless and restful sleep until about two o'clock in the morning, when he automatically awakened for his customary patrol of the remuda. He tugged at the rope which he had attached to his wrist. It had been cut!

Frantically, he leaped to his feet, staring with disbelief at the short length of rope, rubbed his thumb over the cut end, and fought against panic as the full realization of what had happened swept over him.

He looked around for the rest of the horses, but none were there. Only Andy remained. Apparently the wily raiders had realized that taking the bell-mule would make someone notice the absence of the clanking bell. Perhaps they did not want the old mule or believe that he was worth taking.

The worst had happened. Jim had failed in his trust. The drive was almost certain to fail, since only the bare minimum of horses remained. The night herders still had their ponies, and Jim knew that the sleeping drovers each had a horse attached to his wrist. The horse thieves knew that the cowboys would not abandon the cattle to pursue them, even though each of them had only one horse left. It would have been foolish of them to risk capture by trying to steal the remaining ponies, when they could get away safely with the remuda and Nighthawk.

On the cattle drive, each horse traveled much farther than any steer, so the strength and speed of the horses must be conserved for the countless emergencies which constantly required fast action by men and horses. The remaining ponies would be exhausted by the end of the day.

Jim did not know how to handle this emergency. He knew that he should tell Tom Peters or Curly right away. But what could they do? They could not spare men or horses to pursue the thieves. Jim felt that he was the only one available for the job, even though his chances of catching the thieves and recovering the horses were slim. His dread of facing Tom Peters with the news of the disastrous loss left him ready to try anything, no matter how hopeless or dangerous it might be, rather than admit that he had lost the band.

Jim removed Andy's bell, started to put it aside, then changed his mind, muffled the clapper, and tied the bell rope around his waist.

Slinging his rifle across his back, he mounted Andy and started to follow the trail, which was clearly visible in the moonlight. Jim looked back over his shoulder, still hesitant about leaving without first reporting to Tom Peters. Again, he decided against it, promising himself that he would return and face the man who had trusted him to handle an important job. Even if he did not get the band back, he would do that.

## 13

At dawn the following morning, the grim-faced rancher and his drovers studied the tracks left by the raiders and their pursuing wrangler.

"That no-good kid's in on it, too, Tom," Curly insisted angrily. "He skinned out with them ponies just as sure as we're standing here."

"That's foolish talk, and you know it!" Frisco said. "You can read sign. You know somebody stole them ponies when Jim was sleepin'."

"Then why'd he light out? Why didn't he come over and tell us about it, instead of sneaking off like a yellow coward?"

"Hold it, men!" Tom Peters snapped. "Maybe he was

149

afraid to tell us about it, but I reckon Jim's trying to get them back by himself. And the fool kid's apt to get killed doing it. I don't want to hear any more talk against him, until we know for sure he has it coming. A youngster is entitled to make mistakes and to try to make up for 'em. That's how boys get to be men."

The other men nodded their agreement, but whatever Jim's motive had been, the fact remained that the drive would drag to a halt as their remaining horses became tired. The outlook was bleak.

Tom Peters' future depended upon the success of this drive. To lose the herd, or a large part of it, would cost him everything for which he had worked and fought. The theft of the horses placed the rancher in a terrible predicament, but he did not blame his inexperienced young wrangler for the loss.

He could not leave the cattle between two watering places, where it would be impossible for his men to hold thirsty cattle. The longhorns must keep traveling north.

"We'll move the herd up the trail," he said. "Take them to the next water, Curly. Hold 'em there two days; if I'm not there by then, push north again, and I'll catch up with you someplace between here and Abilene."

"You're goin' after the horses?" Curly asked. "They're gone for good."

"Maybe I can find Jim."

"That's a fool play, boss," Curly objected. "He ain't worth the trouble."

"Curly!" Tom Peters' voice cracked like a bullwhip. "You're a good hand with a herd of cattle — maybe the best I ever saw. That's why I pay you top-hand wages. But I don't like the way you deal with men. That boy's doing the best he knows how and he stayed with the herd. He's risking his neck for the brand, and that's the most I can ask of any man. He's going to get equal loyalty from me. Now shut up and move out!"

Blood rushed to the angry *segundo's* face, swelling the veins of his neck and darkening his countenance. He glared at Tom Peters with silent fury, then cruelly dug his spurs into Cutter's flanks and galloped away.

Frisco handed the rancher a package of food, which he had prepared as soon as Jim's absence had been discovered. He knew that Tom would fight against overwhelming odds to protect his ranch and herd, but he would risk his ranch, his herd, and his life for any man of the Tepee brand.

"Good luck, Tom," he said.

"Thanks, we'll need it, Frisco."

Tom Peters rode to the back of the chuck wagon, reached in, and pulled out a short-handled shovel, which he strapped to his saddle. Frisco made no comment. On a cattle drive, men are buried where they fall. The rancher might find Jim too late to do anything but use the shovel and say a prayer.

There were many tracks leading in the direction taken by the horse thieves, but the only tracks Tom Peters needed were the comparatively long, narrow ones left by the mule. Reading sign, back in the dust of the campsite, he knew that Jim had followed the remuda on old Andy.

It was daylight as Tom rode off at an easy gallop

which would cover ground rapidly without unduly tiring his horse.

Jim still had much to learn about driving cattle and about the ways of men of the prairie — both white men and Indians. But he had learned a lot in a few weeks by watching, listening, doing, and asking questions.

"Comanches can get a man so mixed up that he don't know whether he's afoot or on horseback," Frisco had told him. "But they usually don't have to be crafty once they get away with a remuda, because there's not enough men or mounts on a cattle drive to handle the herd and chase after horse thieves at the same time. Once they get away, they ain't likely to be followed any great distance, and they know it."

Jim depended on that fact now. There wasn't time for him to try to outguess his quarry; he had to follow them rapidly and assume that they would not watch their back trail too carefully.

Andy was not fast, but the durable old mule could outdistance most horses with his smooth, ground-covering amble. Jim did not consider his mount a handicap for this job.

Reading sign, Jim could see that the thieves were having trouble with the remuda. His hopes rose. He was gaining on the horse thieves. Excited by the prospect of early success, he urged Andy to move faster. Then he let the mule settle back into his own gait. It was foolish to tire the willing mule needlessly so soon. His stamina might make the difference later on.

It would be even more foolish to risk the possibility of blundering into the hands of the horse thieves. He did not underestimate the marauders' savagery. They had cut his lariat, when it would have been just about as easy to have cut his throat while he slept. But that may not have been for merciful reasons. Perhaps they had let him live because his companions would be less likely to leave the herd to pursue horse thieves than they would to avenge the murder of one of their companions. Out here, they would have no reason to spare his life if they caught him on their trail.

Accustomed to being ridden with neither saddle nor bridle, Andy responded to Jim's guidance until he realized that they were trailing the remuda. From then on, without further direction by his rider, he followed the trail at a steady, smooth gait that tired neither him nor his rider.

Studying the trail as he rode, Jim observed many things which puzzled him. There were stains of a brown liquid in the dust that appeared regularly along the trail. He was sure that they had been left by a man who chewed tobacco, but Jim had never heard of an Indian chewing the stuff. So far as he knew, they used tobacco only for ceremonial smoking. Perhaps Comanches were different from the Indians which he knew. Somehow, he could not visualize any Indian chewing tobacco and spitting the juice. It did not fit, and that bothered him.

Farther along the trail, he saw where one of the thieves had dismounted and left boot prints in the prairie dust. Narrow-toed, high-heeled prints were the mark of a cowboy boot. At least one of the thieves was a white man.

This realization did not comfort Jim. Comanches were reputed to be savage, ruthless fighters and wily horse thieves, but the outlaws who lurked along the cattle trails were known to be far worse. The scum of the earth had drifted to this wild land beyond the reach of law and the rope of the hangman. Murderers, thieves, rustlers — criminals of all kinds — had fled to this lawless territory and found profit in victimizing cattlemen who were too busy to pursue them.

Buffalo hunters, who made their living by the wanton slaughter of buffaloes with their long range .50 caliber rifles, were depleting the herds. Many of them now turned their terrible weapons against the cattlemen — murdering them for their livestock on the way to market, or for their money on the way back. They killed them with the buffalo guns before their victims could bring ordinary weapons within range.

There were those who ran off remudas during the night and hid the horses out so they could return and dicker with the trail boss for a suitable reward for helping to "find the strays." Helpless cattlemen often paid heavy ransoms for the return of their horses, because they could not spare the time to find them and punish the thieves. Frisco had told Jim of some cattlemen who promptly had strung up their oppressors without further provocation, but most of them were forced to pay outrageous prices for the return of their horses. They paid and let it go at that.

Jim knew one thing for sure: he was on a dangerous

mission. He stopped to check the load in his Kentucky rifle, even though he was sure that it was just right. He had never shot a man, but if he had to do it, he did not intend to miss — not when he knew that his life would depend upon his shooting.

Jim studied the trail sign closely. Now he knew that his best chance for success would come by overtaking them at night. They would almost surely observe his approach if he came too close during daylight. If they did, he would be ambushed and gunned down before he had a chance to protect himself.

Observing a dust cloud in the distance, Jim decided that he had come as near to his quarry as he dared. His high-stepping mule kicked up very little dust in comparison with that raised by the remuda, so he held his distance and followed the airborne marker throughout the afternoon. He maintained an interval between himself and the dust cloud that he considered safe, yet reasonably close. Finally, when the sun dropped below the tall prairie grass on the western horizon, and he no longer could feel its burning rays penetrating the red bandanna around his neck, he accelerated his pace and reduced the distance between himself and the telltale dust cloud, until he dared approach no closer.

Oncoming darkness prevented his maintaining the interval that he had been holding. Jim had to close the gap or risk losing contact with the men. He considered leaving Andy at a good grazing place along the way. The rest would do the mule a lot of good, and he could still follow the thieves afoot, just as well as he could on the back of his mule at night. But he noticed that Andy continued to follow the horse trail as well after dark as he had during daylight. The white mule appeared to be fit and certainly was willing to travel, so Jim decided to keep the animal with him.

He dismounted, looped the rope-halter reins around Andy's neck and walked beside him to help conserve the old mule's strength and to stretch his own cramped leg muscles. Jim was a good walker and, fortunately, he was wearing his old shoes rather than the new cowboy boots.

They came to a rise. Jim decided to climb it and to view the area from the vantage point, because his main concern was the possibility of suddenly blundering into the thieves. He left Andy and climbed the knoll, which rose less than fifty feet higher than the surrounding flat land. Before reaching the summit, he saw something that sent his heart pounding with excitement and apprehension.

The small campfire was clearly visible, burning about a half-mile away. He stared at the pinpoint flame, trying to determine the number of men in the group. He was reasonably certain that there were only two of them, but he had to know for sure.

The fire cast too little light for him to scout the enemy from his present position. Jim gripped the stock of his rifle, knowing that he could stalk the men and pick one of them off with a single shot, then get the second one with a throw of his knife — if he worked himself in close enough to them before firing his rifle. He believed that he could kill a man with the knife at a range of twenty-five feet — assuming that he could bring himself around to the decision to kill a man at all. Never having taken a human life, Jim was not sure that he could do so, except in self-defense or in the heat of battle.

If he could make himself think of his adversaries as targets instead of as men, he might be able to shoot before they discovered his presence. He knew that they would not hesitate to kill him. That was the thought he had to hold in his mind as he tried to plan a rapid, surefire attack.

If Jim brought Andy any closer to the camp, one of the remuda horses would surely whinny a greeting to the mule and alert the thieves before he could crawl within the twenty-five-foot zone which he had established mentally as the range within which he must act.

He turned Andy loose where water and grass were abundant. The hungry mule would not stray far. "Get a belly full of this good grass, Andy," Jim said. "We may have to travel fast on the way back."

Jim worked his way toward the outlaw camp slowly and with extreme caution. Stealth was the most important element of his attack at this stage. A wrong move might alert the desperadoes. Time was working for Jim, however, as the men grew more sleepy and less apt to wander out of the firelight.

Not only did his plan depend upon his getting one man right after the other, but he dared not risk the possibility that another one of them might be wandering around and come upon him in the darkness. Once they suspected that they were under surveillance, they could take action. Only so long as Jim retained the advantage of surprise could he choose his own time and method of attack.

The prairie was dark, except for the flickering light of the small fire, but Jim advanced as stealthily as though he were approaching in full daylight. Finally he was close enough to assure himself that there were only two men — both white.

This land was inhabited by men who were rugged and tough; they had to be that kind to survive. But Jim had never seen such mean, degraded faces as those he beheld in the light of the dying fire. He was not altogether sure that he could handle these men, even with his plan of attack.

This pair profited by their cunning, survived through savage craftiness, and they instinctively would be alert at all times. Men like these had to be vigilant, even when they believed that they were beyond the reach of any pursuers. That was their only chance for continued life and freedom. Jim was no coward, but as he studied the faces of these outlaws, he realized that he was afraid of them.

They squatted at opposite sides of the fire, wolfing their food like ravenous animals. Jim thought that he would have very little trouble with his conscience after killing these brutal men from ambush.

Working his way through the grass, foot-by-foot, Jim crawled until he was within twenty-five feet of the closer man. He rested for a minute or two, then sighted down the barrel of his rifle, coolly taking dead aim at the heart of the man who faced him across the fire. He took a deep breath, let about half of the air out of his lungs, and squeezed the trigger to take up the slack.

But his knife was not handy! How could he have overlooked that?

Jim eased the pressure off the trigger, took another deep breath, relaxed, and leaned upon his elbow as he drew the long-bladed, razor-sharp knife from its leather sheath. He stuck it into the ground where he could grab it with his right hand an instant after he fired his rifle. Now he was ready.

Again, he sighted down the long barrel, steadied himself, and started to squeeze, but again, he failed to get a shot off. It was no use! Now he knew for sure that what he had suspected about himself was true. He could not take the life of any human being in cold blood. Maybe the world would be a better place without the two outlaws, but he could not make that decision.

The man he had been about to shoot was now looking straight toward him, staring in his direction with hard, narrowed eyes. Jim knew that his presence was still unknown — but for how long?

What could he do now? Jim was not sure that he could work his way back to a safer position without revealing his presence to the men. Fearfully, he looked around and realized that he had crawled between the men and their gear. They would be crossing the area in which he was hiding when they went after their bedrolls, their tobacco, or for any one of several reasons. He had to get out of there!

Jim had started crawling backward, so he could keep the men within sight, when he saw the handle of his knife silhouetted against the firelight. He crawled back to get it.

"Easy," he silently warned himself. "Take it easy or you're through."

Forcing himself to remain where he was, he fought against the fear which was driving him toward a state of near-panic. Jim watched the outlaws apprehensively. One man suddenly stood up. Jim's heart pounded as he pressed himself flat against the ground, thankful for the tall grass which surrounded him.

Slowly, fearfully, he crawfished away from the outlaws, eyeing them intently, ready for instant action with rifle and knife, if they should discover his presence and attack him. He inched his way around their saddles and other gear and kept crawling until he was sure that he was out of their sight.

Neither Jim's fear nor his inability to kill the men from ambush had diminished his determination to recover the horses. The men of the Tepee spread had to have the cow ponies, and it never occurred to Jim that he might retreat from the outlaws without recovering the remuda.

As Jim watched the two desperadoes, he thought of many plans, but discarded them individually as being too dangerous or too complicated for success. He could not sneak up on the band and release the horses after the men fell asleep. Men who live by stealth are light sleepers. Even a woodsman of Jim's ability could not approach the horses, release the hobbled ones, and drive the band away without awakening these men.

He considered starting a prairie fire to cut the men off from the horses, but that was much too dangerous. A shift of wind direction could back up a grass fire and envelop the remuda in a wall of flames, kill the outlaws, and endanger other men who were herding cattle on the Chisholm Trail. A prairie fire was too terrible a peril to set purposely for any reason.

The men were preparing to bed down. Each of them tied his lariat around the neck of his horse and attached the other end to his left wrist, just as Jim had done. Jim considered the idea of creeping up to the horses, removing the lariats from their necks and attaching them to their saddle horns. Then he could startle the horses and they would drag the outlaws across the prairie before they could gain control of their horses. That would work! Western horses were trained to drag anything that was roped to their saddle horns.

Jim had to wait until he was sure that the men were fast asleep, so he planned while he waited. He knew that he could approach the saddle horses in the darkness without spooking even the shyest ones. Maybe the outlaws' horses were not too high-strung, or the men would not have dared to attach themselves to them with lariats before going to sleep.

Positive that his plan would work, Jim hesitated only because of the possibility that the horses might drag the men to death. It would be a terrible way to die. How could he have the outlaws dragged far enough to gain and maintain complete control over them without killing them in the process?

Being afoot, there was no way that he could stop the horses once they started running. Unless he made both of them run instantly, it was possible that the men might be able to release their wrists before Jim could make his getaway with the remuda.

He wanted to abandon the plan, but he had run out of ideas. He could think of no other way that would give him a chance of success, unless he killed the outlaws in cold blood.

He decided that his plan would work only at dawn, just before the outlaws would normally awaken. He had to prepare for action during the last few minutes of darkness and attack the moment when he first could see clearly. Success would depend upon speed and precision. Someone would surely be killed if he should try it during darkness. He had to wait for several hours.

Meanwhile, how could he keep himself awake? Jim was bone-tired. It had been too long since last he had slept or eaten, and now time was working against him. He was losing strength — the outlaws had replenished theirs with food and were now resting.

Jim had trained himself to awaken after a few hours of sleep, and he had never missed his post-midnight patrol of the remuda, no matter how tired he had been before bedding down. But now he dared not risk the possibility that he might not awaken before dawn. He must manage by what means he could to stay awake all night.

A coyote wailed in the distance, and another one

responded to the weird and mournful cry. An owl hooted softly, and a small animal shrieked as it fell prey to a night hunter. It was a typical night on the prairie. The pattern of life and death went on as it had since life on earth began. Slowly, the stars swung across the sky. The moon rose, brightening the sea of grass.

The night dragged on endlessly for Jim as he used every trick he could think of to stay awake. What he would give for just one hour of sleep! Even fifteen minutes would make all the difference, he thought.

The stars seemed to spin in the sky as he tried to count them. He singled out those which he had come to know well. He found himself thinking about his boyhood in Tennessee, where the stars had seemed less immediate, viewed through leafy treetops.

His boyhood seemed remote and vague — it was so unlike life in the cattle country. But he was so tired now that the present was also unreal, almost as vague as the past. Everything became hazy — as in a dream — even his dangerous mission. And then it became a dream, as fatigue overcame him. Jim slept as the moon drifted across the western sky.

# 14

An icy wind penetrated Jim's clothing, and the cold ground chilled his body. Drowsily, he tried to adjust his bedding, then remembered why there was no bedding. He leaped to his feet and looked about in wild alarm.

It was still dark, but the first glimmer of dawn's light was lifting the darkness from the eastern horizon. Quickly dropping to the ground, Jim looked toward the outlaw camp. He saw that the bedrolls were still spread out, so he warily approached to make sure that the men still slept. Their horses rested quietly.

Daylight would come soon. Jim had to move fast. Cautiously he untied the lariat from the neck of the nearer horse and tied it to the saddle horn. He tightened the cinches. Then he tied the second lariat to the same saddle horn.

Stroking the cow pony's neck reassuringly, Jim bridled the animal without any trouble. Now that everything was ready, he mounted and waited. In a few minutes, there would be light enough for him to see the ground — and the light would awaken the outlaws. The time had come.

He walked the pony out until the slack had been taken out of both lariats, then he dug his heels into the flanks of the horse.

The two outlaws howled, as the lariats violently jerked them awake. They tried to grab their guns, but the painful strain of the ropes against their wrists forced them to clutch the lariats with both hands, while Jim dragged them across the prairie. The young wrangler kept just enough tension on the ropes to prevent either man from getting any slack, but not enough to kill or cripple them. The outlaws threatened Jim and bitterly cursed him.

He dared not drag them very far; no man could survive such an ordeal for very long. He slowed down a little to give the men a chance to rise and walk. The smaller outlaw leaped to his feet and dashed forward, trying to free his wrist. Jim booted his mount, and the two men hit the dirt violently.

"Don't try that again," Jim warned, "unless you want your hides scraped off."

Watching them closely, Jim again slowed down. "Behave yourselves, and you can walk. Act up again, and you'll get dragged. Now both of you hold your free hands high in the air, and I'll let you up; if you want to eat dirt again, lower them just one inch."

The outlaws stretched their right arms above their heads, and he again gave them the slack they needed to scramble to their feet, but not enough to encourage either of them to make a break for freedom. They were pretty groggy from the beating they had taken. Neither man showed any signs of resistance nor tried to drop his right arm, even though it was hard for them to maintain balance walking over rough ground with arms held high. They did not want to be dragged again.

Jim kept them walking at a fast pace. Both had slept with their boots on, as many men did on a cattle drive, to be ready for instant action at any time. So the ground did not cut their feet, but their uncomfortable cowboy boots kept them hobbling miserably behind the fast-stepping horse. Jim curbed his pity. He had no illusions about these men or about what would happen to him if either of his prisoners were to escape and catch him.

An hour passed. The men's threats and curses diminished, then ceased altogether. They were weary and footsore. One of them stumbled, fell, and was dragged until Jim came to a full stop to let him regain his feet.

"Help him up!" he ordered the second outlaw, but the man just shook his head. He was too far gone to aid his fallen partner. They would both have to rest before walking any farther, and that was the way Jim wanted it.

Untying the ropes from the saddle horn, he kept his distance from the desperados, even though both of them looked much too exhausted now to be dangerous.

"I'll leave you here," he said, "and I'll stake your horses out by the creek, about a mile past your camp, on the trail you made on the way there. Just backtrack, and you'll find them."

The men swore at Jim.

"Just for that, they'll be bareback," Jim said. "I'll leave the saddles and bridles back at your camp. Got anything more to say?"

There was no response from either of the weary, battered outlaws.

"You know I'm giving you a better deal than you deserve. I ought to bring the men of the Tepee spread back here and let them string you two up."

He dropped the lariats and galloped off toward the remuda. Looking back over his shoulder as he rode, he saw that the men were too weary to follow him. One man was removing his boots, and the other lay stretched out on the ground. Jim was sure that they were all right, and that they would be in no hurry to follow him back toward their camp. He would have plenty of time to get beyond their reach, but he did not intend to waste any of it.

Most of the band had already converged on Andy by the time Jim got back to them. Finding the rest of them was easy. He released those which were hobbled, and within a few minutes, all of the horses were banded and ready for travel. Jim unsaddled the outlaws' mounts and spread the saddle blankets out to expose their undersides to the sun.

He removed the cartridges from the two guns and from the cartridge belts. He doubted that the outlaws could ambush him before he returned to the herd, but this should discourage them from rustling another remuda for quite a spell. Jim looked admiringly at the pistols, tested their action, wishing they were his. He holstered them and tucked them into the blankets, where they would be protected from dust until their owners returned.

Mounting Andy, he backtracked toward the cattle herd, setting a good, fast pace. He hoped that he would catch up to his outfit shortly after dark.

About a mile from the outlaw camp, he found a good pasture with plenty of water and hobbled the two horses where they would be comfortable until the outlaws found them. The men would be exhausted when they arrived, but their horses would be fresh and well fed, so Jim did not waste any time lingering there. He wanted to put all the miles between himself and the outlaws he could, while he had the chance.

The remuda followed Andy without hesitation as he headed back over the trail. Jim was tired and very hungry, but he could not remember when he had felt better, knowing that he had earned the right to face Frisco, Tom Peters, and the rest of the men without shame.

Before he had gone very far, he saw a man riding up. Thinking it might be another outlaw, Jim dismounted, brought his rifle to the ready position, and waited for the rider to come closer and show his intentions.

The rider hailed him, waving his sombrero. Then Jim recognized Tom Peters. He waved back and eagerly galloped toward the rancher. The remuda followed Andy, making their approach look like a small stampede.

The rancher grinned at Jim. "You're a sight for sore eyes, son," he said warmly. "You and that Andy-mule and your whole remuda. I'm glad to see you."

Jim knew that all was well. "I'm sorry I gave you trouble, Mr. Peters," he said. "I hoped I could get these critters back before you needed them."

"You did fine. Tell me what happened. And here's some chow to hold you till we get back."

Jim related the story as simply and as quickly as he could while they rode.

"And you let the varmints go free?" Tom asked.

"Yes, killing people is a little out of my line, even if they are horse rustlers. And I was afraid to bring them in by myself," Jim admitted. "They're tough hombres. One little mistake would have been my last one. I figured that they'll be plenty weary and footsore before they finish this day."

"That they will," Tom Peters agreed. "But they ought to be strung up. They take a man's mount and let him die out on the prairie without thinking twice. This territory would be well rid of men like that. I reckon somebody else will have to perform that little chore another time. You did well, though, son. Right well!"

They rode together back to the herd, reaching it just as darkness was settling over the prairie. Jim watered his remuda and found a place for them to spend the

night, before he went in for chow, even though they had
enjoyed far more rest and food than he had in the past
night and day. That fact did not pass unnoticed.

"That kid'll do to ride the range with," Tom Peters
said, and Frisco nodded his agreement as he made up a
special plate of chow.

"If he amounted to anything, the horses wouldn't
have been stolen in the first place," Curly growled.

Tom Peters wheeled and angrily faced his *segundo*.
"Whatever you have against that boy, you'd better forget it!" he said. "Jim's earned a place in this outfit, and
I'll back him all the way. Any man who wants to keep
riding for me had better keep that in mind!"

"You're the boss." Curly's voice was flat. He glared
at Tom Peters, put his plate on the chuck wagon tail gate,
and strode away into the darkness.

The cowhands looked at each other, shifted uneasily,
but said nothing, as Tom Peters watched his *segundo* stalk
away. The rancher was just as angry as his top hand was,
but he controlled his temper. His jaw muscles bunched,
then his face relaxed.

Jim arrived at the chuck wagon, unaware of the incident of which he had been the innocent cause. The
grim-faced rancher and the gloomy faces of the men
around him gave Jim the wrong impression. He assumed
that the men were blaming him for having let their horses
be stolen, for subjecting them to the problems involved
in herding longhorns without fresh mounts. He had been
so sure that he had earned their forgiveness that he was
hurt and angry.

"If that's the way they feel, let 'em," he told himself, and he turned away from the chuck wagon and headed back toward his remuda. Hunger and fatigue sharpened the hurt and the disappointment he suffered. He had done his best. If that was not good enough, he'd have to call it quits.

"Where you goin'?" Frisco yelled after him.

Tom Peters understood first. He ran after Jim, grabbed his arm, and led him back to the chuck wagon.

"No, you don't!" he said. "Frisco has a special dinner fixed up for you, and the boys and I want to thank you for a good job. You can sleep later, maybe next fall."

The men gathered around Jim, roughly pounded him on the back, and shook his hand until his whole arm ached. It was an exuberant, rough reception; quite different from the silence Jim had met when first he walked up. Everything was just fine now. Jim was happy.

Famished and fatigued, Jim had just about reached the limit of his endurance, but he was also very proud of his new stature as a man among men and a friend among valued friends.

"Let the boy eat," Frisco pleaded. "Can't you see he's dead on his feet?"

The drovers fell back, made a place for Jim at the fire and hunkered down in a circle around him, pressing him for details about the pursuit, the capture, and the final disposition of the outlaws.

Between mouthfuls of steak, biscuits, and beans, Jim related the story as modestly as he could. But, knowing the love of his companions for a good tale, he did not play it down. As he ate and talked, a feeling of warmth and enthusiasm for his subject gripped him, and he developed a tale far more exciting than the one he had related as a mere factual report to Tom Peters. He did not exaggerate, but he placed the emphasis where he thought it would do the most good. He brought out every detail that would be of interest to his listeners.

"You should've drug 'em all the way back here. If it'd been me on the bitter end of them ropes, I'd have wore them fellers right down to their bones," Moose roared savagely. His ferocious-looking red moustache quivered with excitement. "There wouldn't 'uv been enough meat left on 'em to interest a half-starved coyote."

"Why didn't you keep their horses and guns?" Ace demanded. "I can see where a chickenhearted kid like yourself might not drag them to death, but they sure must have stole them ponies. Nobody'd give it a second thought if you was to take them critters for your own."

"No sense in having horses of my own, when I can't even hang onto the ones I'm supposed to watch out for," Jim said with a grin. The grin gave way to a huge yawn.

"You'd better hit your hot roll, Jim," Frisco said. "You're plumb tuckered."

Jim could not argue the point. It was all he could do to put his plate into the wreck pan, say good night to the hands and unroll his bedding. There was no counting of stars for Jim that night. He fell asleep the moment his head hit the saddle.

# 15

Excitement ran high on the eve of their entry into Abilene. Every man in the outfit was counting the hours and eagerly preparing for the long-awaited event. Frisco baked a huge apple pie in his dishpan to top off a festive dinner that was a short-lived monument to the genius of the trail cook at his best.

After chow, the hands who were not night herding sat around the fire swapping stories and polishing the brightwork of their saddles, bridles, spurs, belt buckles, everything that was silver, or nickel-plated, was polished until it gleamed.

"Well, boys, the Old Man said we'll be in town to-morrow around noontime," Ace said, as he turned a silver-studded spur, first one way then another, to inspect it by the flickering firelight. Finding an imaginary dull spot, he breathed on it and buffed it energetically until there could be no doubt that it was polished to the peak of perfection. "Since we're the first outfit to hit Abilene town with a herd of cattle this year, there'll be a lot of excitement when we pull in."

"We'd better spruce up," Moose said. "Handsome as I am, personally, I reckon I'll take me a bath in the river. Maybe wash all over with soap, even if I don't much need to. I aim to give the town folks a treat and dress up in my best go-to-town duds." Moose was trying his best to trim his magnificent red moutache with the aid of a small metal mirror. But every time he brought the scissors up to clip a few of the luxuriant copper hairs, he found that he could not bear to make the cut. Each time he dropped them away again.

"I already took me a shave," Shorty said. "But you know, I'm a little embarrassed at the idea of going into Abilene town the way things stand right now."

"How so?" Moose asked, his scissors poised in midair.

"I hate to say so," Shorty said, "but Jim here is a Tepee man, and I'll be a mite reluctant to be seen in the company of a young 'un which looks as downright shabby as our wrangler does. I'd feel totally embarrassed."

Jim was astonished. He just couldn't be hearing right! Shorty had been a good friend from the first day they met. Like the rest of the men in the outfit, with the exception of Curly, he seemed like one who would judge a man by what he was — not by the clothes he wore. But

Shorty was apparently dead serious. Jim felt sick.

"Shorty, I shore hate to admit that you're ever right, but this time you hit the nail smack on the head," Moose agreed. "He looks downright shabby. Do you reckon he could ride into town a coupla hours after the rest of us; maybe act like he was from a sheep outfit, or something?"

"We sure don't want to get off to a bad start with the good people of Abilene," Ace agreed. "You're a good enough kid, Jim, but you shore ain't a thing of beauty in those duds. They're all wore out, and you've growed out of 'em in the last coupla months. The way them buttons are strainin' at your chest, you're apt to split wide open at the seams by the time you hit town — and that could be sort of degradin'. Are you sure you don't have some proper clothes stashed away someplace?"

Jim shook his head, not trusting himself to speak. He had planned to buy a new outfit, or as much of it as he could afford, after he got paid and had a chance to shop in Abilene. Now he did not want to enter the town for any reason.

"I'll stay here with the horses," he said, trying to keep the tremor out of his voice. "I don't figure on going to town."

The drovers appeared to be embarrassed as they left the fire, one by one. Even Frisco left, and Jim was alone, feeling miserable. Absently, he finished eating the food that had gotten cold. He did not know what to do. He was too unhappy to sleep, and it was a little too early to make his routine visit to the remuda. He emptied his tin plate and put it into the wreck pan, then he returned to the fireside.

Minutes later, the cowboys returned in a group, but Jim had not the spirit left to look up as he heard them coming. He stared into the flickering light of the fire and kept silent, wishing now that he had left the area so he would not have to face the men he had been so proud to call his friends. Deciding that he could not stay there with them, he stood up and started to walk away. But his path was blocked. Moose looked up into Jim's face and spoke.

"A man's hardly a man at all in these parts, without he's got a Stetson. Let's see how this 'un fits you."

He placed the high-crowned, wide-brimmed, dove-gray sombrero on the speechless Jim's head, adjusted it slightly for a more jaunty effect, then stepped back to admire it critically.

"Mighty handsome," he said. "Just a little dimple here, and you'll look like a real cowhand." He put the dent into the crown and again stepped back to study the effect of his handiwork approvingly.

"That's just fine! Of course, you're not the handsome feller I am, but I want you to have that hat to help make up some of the difference."

"You're giving me this, Moose?"

"Shore," Moose thumbed his old hat back. "That'n ain't used to my head like this'n is," he said. "This'n's like part of me."

Before Jim could thank his friend, Ace stepped up and held a new, blue-flannel shirt with mother-of-pearl buttons all around the shield-front. He shook it out and held it across Jim's chest, looking at it critically.

"That'll fit fine," he said. "You've filled out across the shoulders. This will be just right for you."

Shorty followed up with a hand-plaited bridle. "Nothin' of mine'll fit you, Jim," he explained, "but this'll fit your horse, when you get a horse of your own."

"He's got one," Tom Peters said. "He's got Dancer and the saddle he's been riding since the first day he joined this outfit."

"But Dancer's Frisco's favorite mount," Jim objected. "I couldn't take Dancer away from him. I sure do thank you, though, Mr. Peters."

"Frisco wants you to have him, Jim," the rancher said. "He offered to buy Dancer from me, so he could make you a present of him."

"But the Old Man wouldn't sell," Frisco said, "so I want you to have this Colt. I'll learn you how to handle it on the way back to Texas."

It was a handsome revolver with an open-topped holster and matching cartridge belt. Jim knew very little about pistols, but he recognized the work of good gunsmithing when he saw it.

Jim was proud, happy, and ashamed all at once — ashamed of himself for having doubted his friends during that awful moment when they had deceived him with their elaborate practical joke.

"I sure don't know how to thank you all," he began hesitantly.

"We don't want your thanks, wrangler," Moose said. "All we want is for you to hang onto them hosses so's we can ride into Abilene tomorrow. I'd sure hate to degrade myself by walkin' in."

"Now that you mention it, I don't believe anybody took them ponies," Ace said. "None of us seen any horse thieves — all we got is his word for it. I got it in mind that the kid got a little tuckered and decided to hide out in the brush and catch up on his sleep, while us workin' stiffs trailed the herd in the hot sun."

"But let me thank . . ."

"I don't trust a feller as talks too much," Moose cut in. "The kid's got my best sombrero, and I don't aim to stay here until he talks me outa my britches, too. I'm goin' to bed."

The dust cloud which had marked the herd's progress all the way up the Chisholm Trail signaled its approach to the people of Abilene, and the town rocked with excitement. Jubilant men raced their horses over the prairie to meet the year's first herd of longhorn cattle and escort them to the empty pens.

Tom Peters saw them coming and rode back to bring Jim up to share in the exciting climax of his first cattle drive.

"I thought you might like to get in on this, Jim," he said. "The horses will follow Andy without any trouble for a few miles, and you can go back to them before we get to town."

"Thanks. I'd like that a lot. These fellows look real excited," Jim added as the riders raced toward the herd.

"It's their big day," the rancher said. "The cattle

buyers aren't the only ones who'll gain when they get our herd. Everybody in Abilene will be a little more prosperous before we leave, and soon the town will be overrun with cattle and cattlemen. These ringy longhorns are Abilene's lifeblood."

The men galloped up to Tom Peters and pulled their winded mounts to a dust-clouded, sliding halt.

"I'll buy all you got," the first man boomed. "I'll pay top prices. I've got hard cash, and I'll take the whole herd off your hands — right now, sight unseen!"

"Well, thanks," Tom Peters answered, with a friendly smile. "Let's talk business after we get these longhorns penned. I don't mean to seem uncooperative, but I'd sort of like to get my boys out of the saddle, have a good hot bath, and then make a deal over the biggest platter of ham and eggs in Kansas. I hope you'll be my guest. My name's Tom Peters, and this is my wrangler, and friend, Jim Ryan."

"Pardon my bad manners," the cattle buyer said. "I'm Dan Carlin. I'm apt to get a little excited when I see a big Texas herd. I'd be pleased to join you at the hotel. And I'm glad to meet you, Jim Ryan," he said, shaking Jim's hand with a hearty grip. "You Texans are always welcome here in Abilene town."

Jim immediately liked the bluff cattle buyer — probably partly because Dan Carlin had called him a Texan. He looked the part in the new outfit his friends had given him. He had left the Colt in the chuck wagon, but now he wished that he had worn it for decoration. All of the other men had worn theirs. Then he realized that he had absentmindedly brought along his Kentucky rifle and the sheath knife. "Some Texan!" he thought.

Tom Peters signaled Ace and Curly to swing the herd around the town, but the men of Abilene protested.

"Drive 'em right down the street!" one man yelled.

"We been waitin' all winter for them longhorns, and we want 'em paraded right through town."

"You're going to have a mighty dirty town after twelve hundred longhorns run through it," Tom Peters warned the exuberant townsmen, "but if that's the way you want it, we'll be happy to oblige."

He rode back to instruct the point men and then returned to the head of the procession.

"Do you mind if I take the remuda around town, instead of through it?" Jim asked.

"Don't you want to join the parade, Jim?"

"Yes, I'd like that fine, but I have a feeling this will be more like a stampede, and I don't want any of our horses to get hurt," Jim said. "I want to take 'em all back to Texas in good shape. Besides, the people have plenty of horses. It's the cattle they want to see."

"Okay, Jim. I think you're right. Put the horses away, and I'll see you in town, later. Stop off at the barber shop for a haircut and a hot bath and then meet Dan Carlin and me at the hotel for ham and eggs."

The drovers closed up the herd for better control, so they could drive through town with the least damage to Abilene. The point men held the leaders back, while the flankers and swing men closed up the line and the drags brought up the stragglers.

Jim stood on the bars of the corral in which he had penned the remuda and prepared to watch the passage of the longhorns. He was worried about the idea of routing the spooky animals through town, where any one of a hundred things could happen to frighten them into a stampede. But he realized that the longhorns had grazed well and had been watered that morning. They were just tired enough to be as docile as Texas longhorns ever got to be. So, maybe, he was letting himself get worked up over nothing.

The people of Abilene lined the street, as though waiting to see an Independence Day parade, but the flashing horns and rumbling hoofs of that great herd should have brought doubt to even the bravest of them. The cattle had not seen unmounted people for many months — if they ever had. Driving them through the confining narrow street without knocking over one or more of the rickety-looking wooden buildings or sod-covered shanties seemed like an impossible feat to Jim. He feared for the safety of the happy, excited spectators. His most comforting thought was that this was not the town's first longhorn run. They must know what they were in for.

Curly and Ace handled the point expertly. Big Red was not spooky at the moment. A lot would depend upon how he took to the idea when he entered town. Curly and Ace kept a firm, subtle pressure on him, so he had no time to think up any deviltry. There was little choice for him but to trot right down the middle of the street and, conditioned by habit developed during the long drive up the Chisholm Trail, the others followed Big Red.

The herd rumbled into town, through it, and out of it, and up the road to the stockyards without damaging any property. Jim doubted that there would be dust-free air there for a week or more, but the cheering people did not appear to care about that. Now Abilene would boom again!

And Jim felt just as prosperous and as happy as did the people of the cattle town. He was a working hand with a good outfit. His friends were the best a man ever had, and his future looked very bright. Very bright indeed, for a fellow who had been a sick, lonely stranger just a few months ago. Now Jim belonged. He sat on the corral rail and thought about his good fortune, forgetting about everything else. This was a big moment, and he was enjoying it to the hilt.

Something whistled through the air, and a searing pain ripped across his shoulders as he was knocked from the high rail to the ground. Jarred by the fall and sickened by the pain, he staggered to his feet, shook his head to clear away the fog, and looked into the face of the only enemy he had in the world.

182

# 16

Curly leered at him, standing with his feet widespread, arms akimbo, and with his quirt dangling from his right wrist. He snapped it up, grasping the weighted handle in his right hand, and ran the lash through the fingers of his left hand. His breath reeked of cheap whisky. Curly had gotten his hands on a bottle in a hurry.

"Want another taste of this?" He snapped the lash, and Jim lurched backward just in time to save his face from the heavy whip.

"Scared?" Curly taunted maliciously. "You don't look so good out here all by yourself. You don't hardly stack up like a man at all, when your friends ain't around."

Curly was mean drunk. Jim knew that he could not

183

talk his way out of this situation, and none of the other hands would be coming around to see that this was a fair fight. He was alone with a man who hated him and who was vicious enough to kill or maim him.

Jim's rifle was about fifty feet away. There was no way that he could reach it before Curly could gun him down with his Colt, but at this distance Jim's knife would equalize them. He hated to use it against a man, but he had no choice. Quickly, he grabbed for it — it was gone!

Curly's laugh mocked him. The *segundo* waved the knife at Jim. "Looking for this? I relieved you of it when you hit the dirt. You ain't got nothin' left, nothin' at all."

"That's right, Curly, you've got it all. You've got a quirt, a knife, a gun, and a bellyful of rotgut courage. Too bad you can't get your hands on a cannon and some grapeshot. Then you'd really be brave!"

"I can whip you with one hand tied behind my back on the sickest day of my life, and you know it."

"Prove it. Put away that arsenal and come up looking like a man, Curly." Jim's challenge was hollow, but he had to make Curly put away the weapons, or the cowboy was apt to beat him to death with the quirt.

The *segundo* backed away and began to dispose of his weapons, one by one. Curly tossed his quirt and Jim's knife aside. His laughter mocked Jim, and he shattered the blade with a single shot from his Colt. Then he holstered the pistol, unbuckled his gun belt, and dropped it to the ground.

Jim waited calmly as the man removed his spurs. He had learned about Curly's brutal strength and agility the

184

hard way, and it was obvious that the whisky had not handicapped him. No drunk could have shot the pistol as accurately as Curly just had. Jim had no doubt that he was in for a bad time. This would be a no-quarter fight, whether Jim wanted it that way or not.

He was stronger than he had been on that day when Curly had brutally pounded his face into the dirt. Weeks of hard work and good food had packed solid muscle on his lean frame. But Curly was older, bigger, stronger, and far more experienced as a rough and tumble fighter than Jim, and his vicious cruelty made him a dangerous adversary.

The *segundo* advanced, then stopped about five feet away from Jim and peeled off his shirt, revealing bunchy muscles that rippled with every move of his powerful arms. He laughed harshly.

"Go ahead," he taunted. "Strip down. I'll wait."

Jim could not afford to make a mistake. He trusted Curly to the extent that he would have trusted a rabid wolf. Nothing would make him take his eyes away from his enemy for an instant; nor would he risk the possibility of getting his hands hung up in his shirt sleeves with Curly waiting just one leap away. He watched his opponent warily and waited.

Deliberately, Curly turned away and, with elaborate care, hung his shirt on the corral rail, flicked an imaginary speck of dirt from it, then hung his sombrero on a rail post.

Jim did not take the bait. He just watched and waited.

Curly whirled and leaped with arms outstretched to grab Jim with powerful hands, covering the interval between them in a split second.

Jim sidestepped, just inches, and slammed his left fist into the cowboy's unprotected midsection. All of the power of Jim's muscular body was coordinated into the beautifully timed punch, and to its force was added the momentum of Curly's lunge. The impact drove the air from Curly's abdomen with an explosive whoosh!

The *segundo* dropped to the ground as though he had been poleaxed.

Jim hesitated. In their last encounter, he had made the mistake of closing with Curly after downing him, and the memory of the result of that error was much stronger than his impulse to leap upon the prostrate man and knock him out before he could recover. Jim was not about to fall into the same trap again. This time he erred the other way.

Curly's knockout had been decisive; he was helpless. The paralyzing punch had driven the breath from his body and temporarily immobilized his nervous system. He was at the mercy of his young opponent.

But Jim was not sure. Wary of the strength and savagery of the more experienced fighter, he dared not move in to secure his victory. He waited too long.

Curly was young and tough. For the first ten seconds after the punch had felled him, he lay helpless, without moving. Then, as his strength began to flow back, he sobbed, wheezed, gasped for breath, and writhed in the dust. A half minute after he had fallen, Curly staggered to his feet. Even then, Jim could have finished the fight, but he suspected a ruse.

"That was a lucky punch," Curly croaked as he swayed on widespread feet. "That won't happen again."

He circled Jim, stalling for the time he needed to recover his full strength. Jim saw that color was returning to Curly's face, and now — too late — he appreciated the effect his punch had wrought upon Curly.

Soon the cowboy was ready to continue the fight. He advanced on Jim, crouching, knees bent, with his arms held out in the open-handed position of the rough and tumble fighter, who is ready to punch or grapple, according to the first opening he sees.

Jim backed away, watching, waiting for Curly to come in with a lead that would give him an opening. Curly was protecting his midsection now. A second punch to that region would be doubly damaging, and he knew it. He came toward Jim slowly, ominously crouched low, his jaw buried in his left shoulder, and his forearms held high. His increased respect for the ability of his opponent made him a much more dangerous fighter.

Jim was afraid. The effect of the first punch had not deceived him. Curly was still more than a match for him, and he would try to exact a cruel penalty for the pain which Jim had inflicted upon him. Mere victory would not be enough to satisfy him.

Jim continued to back away, and Curly went after him faster. Then an expression of triumph lighted his eyes. He lunged, grabbed Jim, and rammed his shoulder into his chest, clamping him within the grip of his arms, as Jim lurched back in a vain attempt to elude him.

Jim's feet left the ground as he was driven against the watering trough. Curly pinned him against it and relentlessly bent his spine against the rough edge of the trough. Jim could not resist the force which was straining his back to the breaking point. Curly was going to kill him.

The pressure was unbearable, but Jim remained silent. Neither a plea for mercy nor a cry of pain escaped his lips. He inhaled deeply, in an effort to gather his failing strength. It was a silent, deadly conflict.

But this was not enough to satisfy Curly's vengeance. He would kill Jim, but first he had to make the boy beg for mercy.

Maintaining his leverage on Jim, he slowly brought his left arm around and up to Jim's face. With his right hand, he reached for Jim's hair, so he could hold his head while he worked him over.

Jim felt the changing of Curly's grip and, just before the man could grab his hair, Jim snapped his head forward as hard as he could, driving his skull against the cowboy's nose. The violent blow brought tears of pain to Curly's eyes, forced him to relax his grip for an instant — all the time Jim needed.

He drove both hands against Curly's chest and pushed himself backward into the trough. As he fell, he grabbed his opponent's head, spun sideward, and plunged into the narrow trough with him. Before they submerged, Jim took a deep breath. Curly was taken completely by surprise, and he gasped.

Jim held on, while the cowboy struggled frantically. He knew that Curly's involuntary gasp had cost him a lungful of air, and that was an advantage which Jim intended to use to the fullest. He hung on desperately as he felt his enemy's struggle diminish.

Jim released his grip and pulled the half-drowned cowboy out of the trough, then he staggered and fell in the dust with Curly still in his grasp.

Pounding hoofs made Jim look up just as Tom Peters rounded the corral, leaped from his horse, and knelt beside the exhausted fighters.

"Are you all right, Jim?" he asked anxiously.

"I'll make it," he gasped.

The rancher saw that Curly was coming around.

"I wondered what had happened, when you didn't show up at the barber shop or the hotel," he explained to Jim. "When Curly did not show up to draw his wage-advance, I put two and two together."

Curly coughed up some water, cursed, and tried to stand up, but he fell back in the dust.

Jim stood up and waited for the *segundo's* next move, but Tom Peters took over at that point. "You're through, Curly," he said angrily. "I'm paying you off right now, and I want you to leave town, pronto. I don't want to see you on the streets of Abilene tonight."

The thoroughly beaten bully had nothing to say. He had no fight left in him and no desire to face the men of the Tepee spread. He picked up his gun and belt and his spurs and put them on as Tom Peters watched warily. Curly picked up the heavy quirt, threw it back in the dust and walked away unsteadily without ever looking back.

"He had the makings of a good man," Tom Peters said, "but that mean streak will get him killed before he's much older."

The rancher rode to town with Jim, and, while the boy enjoyed a haircut and a steaming bath, the Old Man arranged to have his clothing dried and pressed. Jim was presentable by the time he walked into the hotel restaurant.

"We're a little early, but Dan Carlin ought to be here in a little while."

"Do you mind if I go over and say hello to Frisco?" Jim asked, as he noticed the cook eating alone at a corner table.

"Go ahead."

"Howdy, Frisco," Jim greeted his friend.

"So you whupped 'im," Frisco said, smiling warmly as Jim grinned at him. "Pull up a chair."

Word of the fight had spread fast.

"When are you heading back?" Jim asked.

"Me and the Old Man figure to pull stakes tomorrow, come sunup. Some of the boys'll stay over a few days and catch up with us on the trail. You comin' with us?"

"Right, and the boss said I'm drawin' cowhand pay now. I got me a promotion, Frisco."

"Well, that shines, Jim! That purely shines," Frisco replied enthusiastically.

"I'll need a lot of help from you. I've still got a lot to learn about driving cattle."

"That you have, and a lot about handling 'em on

the range, too. But you'll make out. You're gettin' real good with a rope; you're as good as anyone in the outfit right now, on account of you practiced all the way up the trail.

"I'll learn you how to handle your gun on the way back. Your good sense showed up when you left it behind today — else you'd be dead right now. You'll make out. You've got a heap of bumps comin', but you'll do fine. You and your Andy-mule will make out real good, cowboy."